PRAISE FOR LESLIE LANGTRY AND *'SCUSE ME WHILE I KILL THIS GUY!*

"With an irreverent, tell-it-like-it-is, suburban-mom-assassin narrator, Leslie Langtry's *'Scuse Me While I Kill This Guy* delivers wild and wicked fun."

—Julie Kenner, *USA Today* Bestselling Author of *California Demon*

"Leslie Langtry has penned a cleverly fresh and glib mystery with just the right touch of romance in *'Scuse Me While I Kill This Guy*....It kept me totally entertained first page to last."

—Tanzey Cutter, Fresh Fiction

D1550974

A KILLER DATE

"Okay, we want details!"

I sighed. "His name is Diego. He's Australian. I met him at the bookstore."

"Ooooh! A man with an accent!" Liv squealed.

My brother rolled his eyes. "And?"

"Well, he's gorgeous as all get out in that tall-dark-handsome kind of way. He's very funny and smart and likes kids. Happy?"

"What does he do for a living?" Dak asked.

And there it was. The little thing I didn't want to tell them. Why? Because there was a teensy, weensy chance that there could be, in the way distant future, a slight conflict of interest there.

"He's a bodyguard." I couldn't lie to them. "But I'm sure it won't be a problem," I rushed to add.

"A what? Gin! Are you crazy?" Dak yelled. "Won't be a problem! He just happens to be a bodyguard in a small city where my immediate family of assassins lives!"

But really, how could that be a problem?

'Scuse Me While I Kill This Guy

Leslie Langtry

LEISURE BOOKS NEW YORK CITY

To Tom, my hero—
        Thank you for making this possible.

To Mom—
        Thank you for making me possible.

A LEISURE BOOK®

August 2007

Dorchester Publishing Co., Inc.
200 Madison Avenue
New York, NY 10016

ISBN-10: 0-8439-5933-9
ISBN-13: 978-0-8439-5933-8

The name "Leisure Books" and the stylized "L" with design are trademarks of Dorchester Publishing Co., Inc.

Printed in the United States of America.

Visit us on the web at www.dorchesterpub.com.

ACKNOWLEDGMENTS

I have to thank my children, Margaret and Jack, for respecting my writing time (not an easy thing for an 8- and 6-year-old to do). A huge thanks to Jodi and Natalie, who kicked me in the ass and got me started. And I can't forget my critique group: Elizabeth, Kim, Susan, Stephanie, Theresa, Jan, Tom, Howard, Jane, Ellen, Gina. And I have to send props to my RWA friends from Phoenix—the RomBabes, as well as Misti and Jen from Ohio and of course, Fredericka from Chicago. Thank you to Leah, my editor, who took a chance on me, and a HUGE shout out to the Scoobies—you know who you are! Thank you to Lori, Beth and Pam for keeping me sane every other Wednesday and to the girls of Brownie Troop #360—you are my inspiration. And last but by no means least, thanks to my cousin Wendy—who totally gets this family thing. You can't pick your family, but I'd pick her.

'Scuse Me While
I Kill This Guy

CHAPTER ONE

"On a large enough time line, the survival rate for everyone will drop to zero."
—**Chuck Palahniuk**, *Fight Club*

No one really liked family reunions. I got that. But when I listen to people complain about it 'round the water cooler, I couldn't help rolling my eyes. I mean really, try it when you come from a family of assassins. Kind of gave "avoiding Aunt Jean's potato salad" a whole new meaning.

That's right. Family of assassins. I came from a line of murderers dating back to ancient Greece. Mafia? Puhleeeese. Ninjas? Amateurs. Illuminati? How pedestrian. My ancestors had invented the garrote, the ice pick, and arsenic. And Grandma Mary insisted that the wheel had actually been devised as a portable skull crusher. I'd tell you the names of some of our famous victims throughout history, but I'd had to sign a confidentiality clause in my own blood when I was

five. So you'd just have to take my word
for it.

I turned the engraved invitation over in
my hands and sighed. I hated these
things. We only held them once every five
years, but for some reason, this time, the
reunion was only a year after the last one.
That meant someone in the family had
been naughty. That meant one of my relatives was going to die.

As I stroked the creamy vellum paper,
for a brief moment I thought about sending my regrets. But only for a moment. After all, it wasn't an option on the R.S.V.P.
card. Unlike most family reunions with
sack races, bad weather and crappy T-
shirts, where to refuse to go only meant
you weren't in the ridiculous all-family
photo, to turn down this invitation was
death. That's right. Death. Any blooded
member of the family who didn't show
was terminated.

Now, where had I put that goddamned
pen? I rattled through the "everything"
drawer, looking for the onyx pen with the
family crest engraved in gold on the side.
It may sound pretty callous to throw a
centuries-old family heirloom in with
tampons, fishing hooks, batteries, and
ten-year-old packs of gum, but I didn't exactly have the usual family sense o' pride.

I found the pen behind some broken
cassette tapes and dusted it off. The coat

of arms practically glowed on the cold black surface. Crossed sabers entwined with an asp were topped off with a vial of poison. Lovely. Really sent that warm homemade-chicken-soup kind of feeling. And don't forget the family motto, carved in Greek on the side, which translates as, *Kill with no mercy, love with suspicion.* Not exactly embroider-on-the-pillow material.

The phone rang, causing me to jump. That's right. I was a jumpy assassin.

"Ginny?" My mom's voice betrayed her urgency.

"Hey, Mom. I got it," I responded wearily. Carolina Bombay was always convinced I would someday skip the reunion.

"Don't use that tone with me, Virginia." Her voice was dead serious. "I just wanted to make sure."

"Right. Like I'd miss this and run the risk of having my own mother hunt me down." For some reason, this would be a joke in other families. But in mine, when you strayed, your own family literally hunted you down.

"You know it makes me nervous when you don't call the day you get *the invitation,*" Mom said, whispering the words *the invitation.* It was a sacred thing, and to be honest, we were all more than a little terrified every time we received one. (Did you ever notice that the words *sa-*

cred and *scared* differ only by switching two letters?)

"I'm sorry," I continued lying to my mother. "I just popped the R.S.V.P. into the mailbox on the corner." And I would too. No point in taking any chances with my mail carrier losing it. That would be a stupid way to die.

"Well, I'm calling your brother next. I swear, you kids do this just to torment me!" She hung up before I could say good-bye.

So, here I was, thirty-nine years old, single mother of a five-year-old daughter (widowed—by cancer, not by family) and still being treated like a child. Not that my childhood had been normal, by any means. You grew up pretty quick with the ritualistic blood oath at five and your first professional kill by fifteen.

To be fair, Mom had a right to be nervous. She had watched her older sister, also named Virginia, get hunted down by Uncle Lou when she failed to appear at the 1975 reunion. That really had to suck. I'd been named after her, which kind of jinxed me, I think.

In case you hadn't noticed, my immediate family members were all named after U.S. states or cities (Lou was short for Louisiana, much to his dismay, and Grandma Mary was short for Maryland). It was a tradition that went back to our first ancestors, who thought it would be a cute idea to name their kids after locations, rather than actual names. My name was Virginia, but as a kid I went by Ginny. Of course, that had changed in college when everyone thought it was a real hoot to shorten my name to Gin. That's right. Gin Bombay. Yuck it up. I dare you.

Bombay had been the last name of my family since the beginning. Women born into the family weren't allowed to change their names when they got married. In fact, the husband had to agree to change *his* name to Bombay. You could guess what happened if they refused.

Non-blooded Bombays were allowed to miss the reunion, as were children under the age of five. Bombays had to let their spouses in on the "family secret" by the time the first reunion in their marriage rolls around. It wasn't exactly pillow talk. And of course, you weren't allowed to leave the family once you knew, or well, you know what happens.

Most of us didn't even tell our spouses until the first five-year reunion. I guess I'd been lucky, if you could actually call it that. My husband, Eddie, had died of brain cancer four years into our marriage. And even though I'd seen the lab results, I still eyed my cousins suspiciously. While

I'm fairly certain we haven't figured out a way to cause cancer, with my family, you never know.

Roma, my daughter, had been born one month after Eddie died. I'd given her the traditional place name, but rebelled against the state thing. I called her Romi. I smiled, thinking about picking her up from kindergarten in a few hours. She was my whole life. All arms and legs, skinny as a stick, with straight brown hair and big blue eyes, Romi had given me back my laughter when Ed passed.

My heart sank with a cartoon *boing* when it hit my stomach. Romi was five. This would be her first reunion. She would have to be drawn into that nest of vipers that is the Bombay Family. Her training would begin immediately after. And in a couple of weeks, she'd go from playing with Bratz dolls to "icing" them. Shit.

CHAPTER TWO

"We are all dead men on leave."
-—Eugene Levine, comedian

The doorbell rang, and I automatically checked the monitor in the kitchen. Yes, I had surveillance monitors. Hello? Family hunts us down! Remember?

"Hey, little brother." Despite my weary voice I gave Dakota a vigorous hug.

"You all right?" he asked more with mischief than concern.

"You're joking, right?" And I knew he was. Dak loved Romi almost as much as I did. He just found the whole family of assassins thing amusing most of the time.

"Well, we went through it and survived. Besides, the training is pretty harmless for the first few years."

"Harmless? That's an interesting way to describe turning your kindergartner into a cold-blooded killer."

"Maybe you could write the guidebook!

The Complete Idiot's Guide to Turning Your Kindergartner into an Assassin." Dak laughed in that easy way he had about him. Single and thirty-seven, he was handsome and funny. And I should mention that he was single by choice. Dak, like most of the people in my family, had "commitment issues." Personally, I thought they took the family motto a little too seriously.

I rolled my eyes. "Yeah. That would work." *Hey!* Was he calling me a complete idiot?

"Look, Ginny, it's not like you can refuse to go." He looked sideways at me. "You are going, right?"

"Duh! Do you think I'm stupid? Like I'd let you raise and train Romi!"

I loved my brother. We were close. We even collaborated on jobs. He had taken this whole *Prizzi's Honor* lifestyle in stride. After three millennia of contracted kills, the family was extremely wealthy, and we all lived off of huge trust funds. In the past seventy-five years, after some smart investing, no one has had to do more than one or two hits a year. So we all lived comfortably. *And* we got Blue Cross and dental.

Dak eased back in the kitchen chair, rudely devouring my Pepperidge Farm Milano cookies. Bastard.

"Look, Ginny, it'll be fine. Romi can handle it."

I shook my head. "That's not all I'm worried about."

He stopped eating, and for a moment I thought I might have a few cookies left. "Oh. The other thing. What's up with that?"

"I don't know. You hear anything?"

Dak shook his head. "I heard Uncle Troy almost got busted in Malaysia last year. But he's on the Council and they don't bust you for *almost* fucking up."

I snatched the Milano bag from him. There was only one left. "Yeah, I haven't heard anything either."

"I guess we just see who shows up and . . ." He gave a dramatic pause a la Christopher Walken, ". . . who doesn't." (Insert creepy "dun, dun, dun" music here.)

I looked at him, and not just as a treacherous cookie thief. "How can you be so cold? We're talking about our family here!"

"And there's nothing we can do about it until it happens. I just hope it isn't someone we like."

Dak was right. If it had to be someone, I hoped it would be one of the more assholish relations. Everyone has someone like that in their family. Right? There are definitely some folks I wouldn't miss too much.

I picked up my cup of coffee. "We didn't mess up in Chicago, did we?" My mind raced to remember the details.

Dakota shook his head, but seemed disturbed. "No. It was a clean kill. Nice work, by the way."

"Thanks." Our hit had been screwing so many married women that there were plenty of suspects in his death. Of course, we'd done such a good job, the police didn't even consider murder. I smiled, remembering painting the inside of the chain-smoking son-of-a-bitch's condoms with pure nicotine—which, of course, killed him. That was fun. Rolling each condom up and putting them in the bags so they didn't look "tampered with," on the other hand, was not.

"Maybe it's nothing," I murmured. "Maybe they're going to give us an earlier retirement age." Who was I kidding? Bombays are allowed to retire at fifty-five, although most don't. I mean, Grandma was pushing eighty, and just last week she rubbed out a made man in the Sicilian mob. There's definitely something to be said for loving what you do.

Dak laughed. Pushing a stray lock of sand-colored hair off his forehead, he replied, "Could be Uncle Lou has found a new poison."

I perked up. Poison was my specialty. Everyone in the family had a favorite way of killing people, even though we were required to cross train. With my brother, it was asphyxiation and/or strangulation. And while I should probably worry about that, it made us a good team because we both liked to make each job resemble death by natural cause. Of course, occasionally we ran out of time and had to leave the scene of the crime with a plastic bag still on the victim's head, but that happened only once when I'd been running late from picking up Romi from preschool. And Romi always came first. I had to have my priorities straight, after all.

Most gigs took place in other parts of the country. We had to maintain discretion. But occasionally, the job had to be local. We were *supposed* to get more time to plan those. Oh well, Murphy's Law, blah, blah, blah.

"I haven't heard any gossip," I said absently.

"Maybe with Delhi turning fifteen, and Alta and Romi turning five, they just want to focus on the ritual?" Dak offered, albeit not helpfully.

"I don't know . . . they've never done that before." And there it was. My baby would learn about the family. She'd start practicing with the chemistry set and sniper rifle that came standard with the

blood oath. Ooooh, I hoped she would get
the new, tricked-out Remington with laser
sites! What? It wasn't different from first
communion, a bat mitzvah or quinceañera.
Right?

Dak slapped the table, startling me
into spilling my coffee. "Well, there's
nothing we can do about it until we get
there." He rose and kissed me on the
cheek. "I gotta run. I need a new swimsuit for the trip." He punched me in the
arm and left with a wink.

I guessed I'd have to start packing soon.
The reunions were always held at Santa
Muerta, a private island the Bombays
owned off the coast of Ecuador. Hmmm,
the weather would be hot. And as beautiful as it was there, I wasn't sure I wanted
the family to see me in a swimsuit.

Who was I kidding? Everyone was going
to be way too paranoid to notice I'd put
on a few pounds. And then I thought
about Romi.

Picking up the phone, I called my
cousin Liv (short for Liverpool, if you're
keeping tabs on the place-name thingy.
And if anyone had a right to hate her
name, Liv took first prize). She answered
on the first ring. The Bombays practically
invented caller ID.

"You got it?" she asked breathlessly.

"Yup. You?"

"Yeah. I'll be over in five." On that, she hung up.

Actually, she made it in four minutes flat. Assassins really know how to kill time. (Sorry. I couldn't resist.) I let her in and we went into the kitchen, where I poured her an iced tea.

I loved my kitchen. I hated cooking, but I loved the kitchen. Considering that I dealt in death so much, I had filled the room with bright, cheery colors. The paint was yellow, and the curtains and potholders were citrus green. It was the room of my denial. And for me, sometimes denial was better than most orgasms. Not that I had been on the receiving end of an orgasm in a while. Try years . . .

Liv sipped her tea, then set it down. "I hate this."

I nodded. "Me too."

"I'd say it's not fair, but there's nothing I can do about it."

"Well, we went through it and survived," I mused, realizing I was parroting Dak's words.

Liv shook her head. "I never wanted this for Alta."

"Woody took it in stride . . ." I started.

She raised her right eyebrow. "I know, but he's a boy. I don't mean to sound sexist, but they're different." She wisely avoided looking at me (I hated that "boys are different" crap). "So you're okay with it?"

"Not really. But there's no alternative."

And there wasn't. Things are pretty black and white when your options are either live or die. And as far as I knew, no one had ever tried to get their kid out of the ritual.

Liv tapped her fingers on the counter, her eyes a million miles away. She was gorgeous, kind of in an earth mother/cold-blooded assassin sort of way with long black hair, soft brown Bambi eyes (that could turn you into stone when she was pissed off), and no makeup necessary. Who else would name her kids Woodstock and Altamont? She specialized in political kills. Especially neoconservatives. I kind of envied her that. Lately, I'd just been getting crooked lobbyists and tobacco execs. Booooorrring.

Liv and I had always been close. Being the same age will do that. Her husband, Todd, was one of my best friends. He was a great guy, funny and smart. He was laid-back, not minding the family business at all. Marrying a Bombay hadn't changed him.

"What does Todd think?"

Liv smiled. "He's spent years preparing for this day—the day his baby girl becomes a professionally trained killer. He's

more interested in her survival than anything else."

I nodded, "Since we have to do it anyway,
maybe we can train them together. . . .
You know . . . ease them into it gently?"

She perked up. "Okay. Maybe we can
work something out."

While most women sitting in a kitchen
might discuss the weather, local schools
and Oprah, we chatted for about an hour
about a new garrote Liv had come up with
that didn't leave telltale lines on the victim's throat. Earth-mother beauty or not,
that girl was as strong as an ox when it
came to throttling someone. We avoided
the "other issue" of which family member
had a target painted over his or her picture in the Portrait Hall of Santa Muerta.
It wasn't really coffee klatch material.

"Let's have lunch tomorrow," she suggested as she ran out the door.

Sure, I thought as I rinsed the glasses
in the sink, she had a husband to help
ease the guilt. I had to make the decision
myself.

What was I thinking? Of course Romi
would take the blood oath. I wasn't going
to risk her life for a simple bloodletting
and do-it-yourself murder kit. (Especially
if it included the new Remington S-2000.
Yum.) Besides, it would be ten years 'til
her first kill. So I had some leeway there.
I shoved these thoughts aside.

I had something more important to worry about: the reason for the quickie reunion, basically. I did a mental head count of the thirty-five blooded members of the Bombay clan. But nothing remotely resembling an idea came to me, so I gave up.

I resigned myself to waiting. Well, and mapping out the basement to prepare for Romi's training. I made a list of things I would need: fifty-pound heavy bag, strong piano wire, archery set, mannequins and night-vision goggles. They were put on the shopping list next to potatoes and milk. I could stash the chemistry set in the corner, near the windows for ventilation. But I didn't have a room long enough to shoot a .22 sniper rifle.

With a sigh, I opened the phone book to find shooting ranges. I had a lot to do today, and finding a swimsuit that would take off twenty pounds simply wasn't on the list.

CHAPTER THREE

"You can always count on a murderer for a fancy prose style."
—Vladimir Nabokov

Borders Books was, as usual, crowded. I tried the search computers to find a book in the children's area on assassination, but came up blank. I guess that shouldn't have come as a surprise. What did I expect? Titles like *Harold and the Purple Silencer, Good Night Moon . . . Sleep with the Fishes*, or *Dick & Jane Poison the Federal Witness*?

I ducked into political science and scanned the titles, looking for something simple, like a pictorial guide to assassination. I found one book, but it was all amateur hits like John Lennon, President Ford, and Abraham Lincoln. Oh well, I guess that would have to do. The photos weren't too gory, and they had the Rasputin story (one of my personal faves) in there, so I thought it might work.

"Excuse me," purred a male voice with a thick Australian accent.

"Oh, sorry. I'm in the way." I turned to see who had the delectable, come-hither voice and found myself face to face with the most gorgeous man I had ever laid eyes on.

"No, you're okay. I just wondered what time it was." He smiled, and I melted into an embarrassing, oozing puddle.

"Um." I looked at my wrist. "eleven-thirty." How's that for sparkling conversation?

He grinned, his eyes wrinkling in the outer corners, and I thought I was gonna die. "Thanks."

Look for a ring! Look for a ring! I had the ability to observe things so discreetly no one knew I existed. Unfortunately, hot Aussies tripped up my mojo. I was convinced he saw me look at the ring finger of his left hand.

"Sure. Anytime." *Anytime? What the hell does that mean?* I wouldn't mind running into him anytime, but I was making no sense. *Mental note—don't accept jobs where you have to hit men who have accents.*

The God-Among-Men (I had the habit of giving people names with a Navajo kind of ring to them) laughed and walked away. I just stared with my jaw open until he disappeared. Grace Kelly, I was not.

An hour later, nestled in the corner of the café with a huge slice of Death by Chocolate cheesecake (I love that name) and a large mocha latte, I found myself wondering if I really could kill someone with chocolate cheesecake. No, that would be a waste of perfectly good chocolate. Most of my hits didn't deserve to die so richly.

"Interesting books you have there." The Aussie was back.

I looked around. No, he was definitely talking to me!

"May I join you?" he asked. "There are no other open tables, and I'm intrigued by your reading list."

I nodded like a bobble-head doll, and he pulled up a chair.

"Diego Jones." He held out his right hand, and I took it.

"Ginny Bombay." I returned his shake and felt my cheeks go hot as he examined my boobs . . . I mean books.

"*Political Assassination, Assassination through History, Encyclopedia of Assassins*," he read through the titles casually, "and *Assassination Vacation*?" He held up one book.

"Oh, that's by Sarah Vowell. She's one of my favorite writers." It was true. I'd loaned my copy to Dak, and he promptly lost it. It was a very funny book about her pilgrimages to presidential assassination locales. I liked funny.

"So," Diego began, "Ginny Bombay?"

I braced myself to hear the same joke I'd heard for the past . . . well hell, all my life.

"Would that be short for Virginia?"

What? A real conversation with no joke regarding the implied alcoholic content of my name? I should jump him before he realized what an idiot I was.

"Wow. You're good. Most people come up with something far more lame when I introduce myself."

Diego laughed again. "Not me. My mum was eccentric in choosing her kids' names too."

"Oh, really?" I tried to act casual as I unwittingly sprinkled salt into my latte.

Diego raised one eyebrow. I casually set down the saltshaker as if it were the most natural thing in the world.

"Mum was an artist back in Sydney. She had a thing for the Mexican muralist, Diego Rivera. My sister got it worse. She's Frida Kahlo Jones."

I laughed. "My family is hung up on place names. My brother is Dakota, and my mom is Carolina."

He chuckled, with those delightful wrinkles at the outer corners of his eyelids. I tried very hard not to swoon. At least, not obviously. He was perfection.

Dark, wavy hair, cool James Dean side-
burn slivers, smiling blue eyes and gorgeous white teeth.

Diego took a forkful of salad, and I fantasized about being that fork—especially
having his tongue slide over my tines.

"So why this particular subject?" He
gestured toward my tower-o-terror.

Fortunately, I wasn't too distracted. I
went into cover mode, telling the story
I'd used for years. "I'm in executive protection. Just occupational curiosity, I
guess." Claiming to be a bodyguard had
worked well for me over the years. It explained my bizarre reading habits and
chaotic work schedule. Yep, my cover
had always been 100 percent reliable and
unshakeable.

"No kidding? That's what I do!" Diego
grinned.

Okay, not so unshakeable. "Really?" I
asked, hoping he was teasing me. I'd
never met any bodyguards in person before. I usually just had to slip around
them unnoticed. Well, there had been
that one time when Dak and I had gotten
jobs *protecting* our hit. That had been
hysterically ironic.

Diego nodded. "Absolutely. Who do you
work for?"

*Calm down, Gin. Just use the patented
answer.* "A motivational speaker on the
East Coast. You?" Nice transition.

"I've worked for political clients mostly." He went on to name a number of senators, mayors of major cities, and the like. He seemed legit. I was just grateful none of the names had been on my list in previous years. "So I understand your area of interest." He pointed to the books. "I'm kind of an assassination nut myself."

I leaned back in my chair, appraising the situation. That was what we did, by the way—appraise situations. You didn't think we just barged in and gunned people down, did you? No, that'd be soooo Squeaky Fromme. I decided that Diego was definitely safe to talk to and certainly a candidate for some killer sex.

"So what's your favorite assassination in history?" I asked. I never got to ask civilians this question. This could be fun.

Diego looked to his right, deep in thought. "I guess it would have to be Kennedy. All that conspiracy stuff is pretty interesting."

I smiled. I knew who had been on the grassy knoll that day. Assassination tales had been my bedtime stories.

"Too recent for me," I responded. "I like the questionable cases too, but further back. I prefer Philip of Macedon."

"Ah." His gravelly accent sent shivers down my spine. "Murdered at his daughter's wedding reception. I thought they knew who did that."

No one knew that. Well, except the thirty-five members of the Bombay family. It had been on a test we had to take when we turned ten. Let's just say that another guy took the fall for that particular assassination. Rule #1: If you can make it look like someone else did it, go for it.

"That's what some historians think."

"And you know the truth?" Diego-My-Love responded. I pictured myself licking every square inch of his body.

"Of course not," I said. "That's what makes it my favorite."

"I like you, Ginny Bombay." Diego leaned back in his seat. "You're not like other women."

You have no idea. "Sure I am," I said. "Just like all the other female bodyguards you meet at Borders."

Diego shook his head. "No. You actually eat." He pointed to my dessert. "And I've never seen anyone salt their latte before."

My mind scrambled for purchase on slippery thoughts. "Oh, that. I do that to counter all the sweet stuff." Nice try. But the latte was terrible with salt in it. Really, don't try it. Assassin fun fact #1: Did you know you could kill someone with a simple overdose of table salt?

"I hate it when women eat only salads and fruit. It's not right," Darling Diego continued.

"Well, you know what Erma Bombeck

said," I responded. "Never turn down dessert. Think of those poor women on the *Titanic* who waved away the dessert cart."

Diego laughed. It was amazing. I made him laugh. It was the most incredible feeling of euphoria, and I wondered how I could get him to do it again.

"Just one thing," he asked. "Who's Erma Bombeck?"

I rolled my eyes. "A woman writer. She was very funny."

"I don't care who she is," he said, "I'm just happy to see a woman who enjoys her cake."

I chose not to be offended by the remarks of the future Mr. Ginny Bombay. "Good. Now prove you're not a hypocrite and go get yourself one." I pointed to his salad and whole-grain bagel with veggie cream cheese. "Cuz that is not food."

He leaned forward, eyes twinkling. "Only if you will wait for me." I think I nodded or something because he laughed and walked to the counter. I'm pretty sure it took all my faculties not to be naked when he returned.

And so for the next two hours, Diego and I had a great time. We talked about nothing really, and yet the conversation seemed so profound. At least, I think it was. It was all I could do not to hit him over the head and drag his unconscious body to the nearest hotel. Not that I'd ever done that.

Imagine my horror when I looked up at the clock (the only time I took my eyes off him, I might add) and saw I had only ten minutes to pick up Romi from school.

"Shit! I've gotta run!" I said gracefully, as I shoved my books back into the bag.

"Wait," Diego protested. "Here's my card. Call me and I'll take you to dinner."

"Deal!" I shouted over my shoulder as I ran from the store. I slipped the card into my pocket, threw my things into the minivan and raced to Kennedy Elementary.

Romi ran from the door of the building into my arms. She weighed next to nothing but always managed to knock me back a few steps. I didn't mind. In fact, her strength would be a benefit to her training. *Did I really just think that?*

"Virginia!" A booming contralto filled the air. I watched as the other parents scattered as soon as they heard the woman's voice. Cowards.

Great. Vivian Marcy. I really hated that bitch. President of the PTA, member of the school board, and for some reason, Romi's room mom. I had grown up with Vivian Marcy. We'd been in the same class in school, and she'd been an evil witch

there too. For years I'd prayed she would
turn up on my hit list.

Unfortunately, Vivian still hadn't pissed
off anyone enough to warrant a death
contract. On several occasions, I thought
of taking one out on her myself, but figured I'd get busted. Bombays aren't allowed to come up with the targets, unless
it's family. Still, hope springs eternal.

I knew I wasn't the only one who hated
her. Since childhood she had spread her
withering gaze like a thick layer of rancid
mayonnaise. (Hey! That kinda rhymes!)
The bitch dominated everyone around her.
I had stood up to her once, early in my elementary school years. She'd managed to
spread the rumor that I had syphilis
cooties. None of the other second graders
had known what that was, but they were
convinced they'd catch it if they talked to
me. So I'd punched Vivian in the nose at
recess. The next day, she had come down
with a raging case of chicken pox, or as my
classmates insisted—syphilis cooties.

While I'd enjoyed the fact that kids had
been afraid of me, let's just say I didn't get
a lot of play dates. Fortunately, I'd had
Dak and Liv.

My dream hit would be to give Vivian
syphilis cooties. A real mean, permanently scarring kind that would give her
eternal body odor and halitosis. Of course

it doesn't exist, but I keep the candle of hope burning.

"Well," Vivian said as she closed in, "if it isn't Virginia. Just who I was looking for."

CHAPTER FOUR

"Well, dear, for a gallon of elderberry wine, I take one teaspoonful of arsenic, and add a half a teaspoonful of strychnine, and then just a pinch of cyanide."
—**Martha, *Arsenic and Old Lace***

No one, and I mean no one, called me "Virginia." Even my family respected that. Well, except for Mom. And if you saw her practicing with her throwing knives, you'd let it slide too. Somehow, Vivian had zeroed in on this when we were kids and did it just to piss me off.

"What do you want, Vivian?" I said in clipped tones, hoping she would get the point.

She didn't. "I need you to bring four dozen cookies to the Halloween party."

Inwardly, I groaned. Outwardly, I think I smiled, kind of like a dog when you can't tell if it's smiling or snarling. "But that's six weeks away. Why not tell me later?"

Vivian arched her perfectly waxed right eyebrow. "I just wanted to make sure you bring home-baked cookies, not just something you pick up at the last minute at Hy-Vee."

"What?" My fingernails carved into my palms. I toyed with hitting her in the nose again. Maybe she would get chicken pox this time too.

Vivian Marcy crossed her arms over her St. John velvet jogging suit. "It just seems more homey and personal when you actually put in the work, that's all."

Put in the work? "Vivian, they're five. They don't know or care if the cookies are homemade."

"Really, Virginia." She actually rolled her eyes, "I'm not asking for much. Just some cookies decorated like ghosts. That's all!" She glanced down at Romi, who was eyeing her with suspicion. Good girl. "I have to go. The PTA's executive officers are meeting in a few minutes. Don't forget. Homemade cookies." With a departing smirk, she turned on the heels of her Prada sneakers and headed back into the school.

"Mommy?" Romi asked. "Is it okay if I don't like her?"

I took her hand and squeezed it lightly. "Yes, honey. In fact, I think that's just fine." Okay, maybe not the most mature response, but I didn't care.

Back at home, my super-intuitive daughter and I had our snack, followed by work on a shoebox she had to decorate for school. By five o'clock, she was happily watching her favorite cartoons, and I was whipping up a gourmet batch of frozen chicken nuggets and french fries for dinner.

You might think that being a stay-at-home mom, I'd be a little more conscientious when it came to dinner. Not me. I hated cooking. Really. In fact, Vivian's request—no, demand—that I make and decorate four dozen cookies really set me off. Of course, I would buy them from a grocery store. Just because she ordered me to do something didn't mean I'd do it. I had my dignity after all. Plus, thinking of Vivian's words would be inspiration during my next hit. That made me smile.

"Mommy?" Romi asked while we snuggled on the couch to watch *Survivor, Arctic Circle*. I suppose you think it's bad to allow your kid to watch TV, but I found this particular show educational.

"What?"

"Alta said we're going on vacation soon. Where are we going?"

"Well," I said slowly, "we're going to an island in the ocean for a family reunion."

"Oh." Romi turned her attention back to *Survivor*, laughing as the contestants tried to start a fire in the snow. I mean, it wasn't as sexy as the more tropical versions of the show. It's kind of hard to get a tan and run around scantily clad in the snow and ice. I was hoping they'd have to dodge a hungry polar bear or at least a rabid harp seal before the season ended.

Later that night, as I collapsed on the couch, ignoring the dirty dishes and baskets of unfolded laundry, I felt a wave of relief that Romi hadn't asked more about our upcoming trip.

What should I tell her? Eddie had always been good at this kind of thing. A stab of guilt hit my stomach when I realized I'd never told him the truth. He had accepted taking on the family name with no problem. I guess when your name was Johnson, anything else looked good.

Damn. Much as I'd like to avoid it, I'd have to tell Romi something. But what? What had Mom told me? I had no memory of that. It was as if I'd been born knowing that nunchucks and plastique were in my future.

There were parenting books on potty training, raising polite children, and so on, but nothing for this problem. Maybe I could manage somehow. For thousands of years, my family had transferred our history to each new generation. What did they do?

Looking at the clock, I saw it was too late to call Mom, Liv or Dak. I turned off the TV and took a book up to bed. Light reading would take my mind off it until tomorrow when I could actually do something. Curled up with a pillow and blankets, I opened my book and within minutes I was laughing my way through *The Dead Zone* by Stephen King. I loved that book.

CHAPTER FIVE

[A grenade lands at his feet] "And everything seemed to be going so well."

—Dwight, *Sin City*

If you were to stand in front of my house, you would: (a) not see my secret attic, and (b) draw the attention of my surveillance monitors, making me very, *very* nervous. But let's go with the first thing, shall we?

I had a lovely Victorian house in the Queen Anne style. Behind the low-pitch, center gabled roof was a hidden dormer room, my secret workshop.

When I'd bought the house, I'd been single and fresh out of college. (I had majored in Russian Lit. and minored in botany. More on that later.) Because of my unusual family business, I had hired a carpenter/electrician from Chicago to put in a "special room" for me.

Bombays are supposed to be extremely discreet. So I had thrown an insane amount of cash at the guy I picked for the job. After exhaustive research to discover that he worked alone and moved around a lot with no family commitments, I'd hired him and sent a limo to pick him up. Of course, the limo driver had been Dak, who had given him a cup of coffee laced with one of my special knockout drugs. Robby Carmichael hadn't known what hit him. He had woken up in St. Louis . . . or rather . . . he *thought* he'd awoken in St. Louis.

Instead, he'd been here. I'd put him up in the guest room, and he'd begun work immediately. My cover story had been that as a single woman, I was incredibly paranoid and wanted a secret "safe room." Robby hadn't watched TV, listened to the radio or gone out. He simply ate, worked and slept. Those had been the conditions of his job, and I paid him well.

The whole time he'd been here, I wore a wig, fat suit, brown contact lenses and several facial warts. I'm sure he'd wondered why I needed a "safe room," considering my appearance, but to his credit, he had never asked. Once he'd been done, I killed him so no one would know I even had this room.

Just kidding. Bet you thought I really iced him, eh? Nah. I had just rendered him unconscious and had Dak deliver him home. He had woken up in his bed, none the wiser and a whole lot wealthier.

The secret room was completely white,

with a ceramic tile floor. The ceiling had skylights disguised as solar panels. There were ten different surveillance monitors on the wall opposite the door.

Metal bookshelves took up the rest of the space, filled with jars labeled with numbers. This system made sense only to me. There was a small desk with a laptop computer and one of those really cool, ergonomic task chairs from Levenger's.

Bolted to the floor, in the middle of the room, were two lab tables and a sink littered with beakers, test tubes, a microscope and slides. There were no personal effects, except for a poster with a kitten dangling from a branch and saying "hang in there." My mom had given it to me when I started training.

Anyway, my daughter didn't know about my workshop yet. Why not introduce her? (*Romi, this is Mommy's death lab. Death lab, Romi.* Actually, she'd probably like the kitten poster.) I don't know. She thought of me as her mother: bedtime storyteller, owie-kisser, cuddler. I wasn't ready to reveal that other side to her. It was schizophrenic, but that's what made it tolerable. There were two Gins: one who was a model mother, perfect daughter, etc. And one who could hogtie a man in such a way that the slightest release of tension in the rope could break his neck. That had taken all of my sixth-grade year to learn, by the way. And there were *no* merit badges for that kind of knot-tying in Girl Scouts. Believe me. I checked.

My lab was so well-concealed that my late husband hadn't even known it was there. Of course it helped that he had been oblivious to anything outside of his den. He had once gone three weeks without noticing that I bought all new furniture for the living room. In fact, I had to tell him. Compare it to the day I had borrowed his letter opener (not for a job, but to actually open letters) and laid it on his desk instead of placing it back in his cup. The man had freaked out.

Of course, I had loved that about him. I had loved everything about Ed. He'd been smart, quirky, funny, and he'd had the loveliest blue eyes. And when he laughed at one of my jokes, I swear I levitated off the ground with euphoria.

Where was I? Right. My lab. Anyway, the laptop was my entire office. Grandma Mary would kill me (if I have to explain it at this point, you haven't been paying attention) if she knew how much stuff I had in there, including files on every member of the family.

That was where I found myself the next morning after Romi went to school, sitting at my desk, checking up on the Bombays. I thought if I could figure out who was going down, I might have an edge. Even with family, you can never have too much leverage. And I have to admit I was a little worried for my own immediate family. Common sense told me none of us was in danger. At least I think that's what common sense was telling me. Either that, or I was hungry.

Deciding not to take chances, I locked up and hit the kitchen. Two Ding Dongs and a half can of Pringles later, I threw on a jacket, grabbed my purse and headed out the door. Whenever I felt overwhelmed or on edge, there was one place I could go to relax.

"Hey, Ginny!" Vera looked up from the register.

"Anything new, Vera?" I asked hopefully.

The old woman threw her thumb over her shoulder. "Yup. In the back. Help yourself."

"Thanks." I headed to the back of the shop. Vera always had something special for me when I came in, which was often. She ran the best pet store in town.

"I thought I'd find you here." Dak's sudden appearance made me jump.

I made a face. "You know me so well."

He knelt down beside me. "Maybe, but I'll never know why you come here so often."

"Well." I sighed, peering into the large, glass case. "It's therapy really. Calms me down."

Dak tapped on the glass. "Why don't you just get one of these guys?"

Good question, I thought as the puppies raced over to inspect Dakota's finger. Why didn't I get a dog? I love dogs! And I would achieve godlike status in Romi's eyes.

I rose and lifted the lid of the box, carefully scooping up a pug puppy. Vera always let me handle them. Not many people were allowed to. But I came regularly, and once I had roughed up two goons who were bothering her, so I guess that made her trust me.

In spite of what I do, I would never, ever hurt an animal. Not that I've ever been asked to. No Bombay has ever killed an animal, as far as I know. (Well, there was that gorilla, but he had known sign language, and we just couldn't leave witnesses behind, could we?) Of course, it may have something to do with the fact that animals don't sell guns, drugs, or spill their guts to the wrong people. Unless you're a signing gorilla. And trust me, he'd had it coming.

"I don't know," I said in response to Dak's question. "It's a lot of responsibility. . . ."

"And being a single mother isn't?"

I shook my head. "Look, I can manage to keep myself, a child and a backyard full of plants alive. I don't think I can add one more life form to that equation."

"Okay, Mr. Spock." He laughed and took the squirming pup from me.

"You're right, I guess." I sounded like an idiot. There was really no reason not to get a dog. The pug struggled in my brother's arms, trying to get back to me. I lifted her to my face and a licking frenzy commenced.

"You know what?" I said, more to myself than anyone else, "I'm gonna buy you. Right now!"

And that was just what I did. Dakota helped me fill a shopping cart full of puppy food, toys, and a small crate. I handed Vera my credit card, and she smiled.

"Finally! After all these years, I never thought you'd do it!" she teased.

"Well, I had to do something at some point or you'd ban me from the place. Besides," I looked at the snoring pup in my arms, "how can I resist a girl who snores?"

Back at the house, I felt a spring in my step. I was happy, giddy really. Dak and I set up all of Poppy's stuff. That's what I named her, Poppy. It was kind of a sentimental botanist/assassin thing. Soon we were sitting in the living room, my newest purchase happily sleeping in my lap.

"So," I finally asked, "why'd you come looking for me, anyway?"

Dak's smile faded a bit as he reached into his jacket and pulled out a large manila envelope.

My mouth dropped open. "I have an assignment? Now?"

He nodded. "Yup. Mom dropped it off this morning."

"Dak!" I screamed. "I don't have time for that now! With the reunion coming up, having to tell Romi about everything and four dozen ghost-shaped cookies to bake! Why did you let me buy this dog?" I felt more than a little betrayed.

He raised his hands against my outrage. "Whoa! Don't shoot the messenger! It's just a job. I thought maybe getting Poppy would help relax you, is all."

"What!" I seriously considered shooting him. "How can I relax now? Oh my God! I wonder if Vera will take her back?"

I looked at the little dog, curled up in my lap, oblivious to my rantings. She was awfully damn cute. What the hell was I going to do with her? And the reunion was coming up! What was I thinking?

"Calm down, Gin!" Dak smiled that big, toothy smile that peeled clothing off young blondes. "You need some sort of break. You don't have to do the job right now. You know that."

He was right. I had at least a two-week window. But with that damned reunion coming up, there wasn't much time to prepare.

"And you know Dad or Todd will watch her. They never go to Santa Muerta." He looked at his watch. "Ooh. Gotta run, Sis. I've got a date tonight."

I nodded weakly as he let himself out. Oh sure, he had a date. I had an untrained, narcoleptic puppy and an oblivious kindergartner. Dak was probably meeting some hot chick for dinner somewhere nice. Bastard. I never got to do that. And while I didn't necessarily mean I wanted a hot chick, anything would be an improvement over my current celibacy situation.

Something clicked in my frazzled brain. I gently placed Poppy on the couch and retrieved my purse. It was still there! I walked to the phone and dialed the number on the card.

"Hello?" that hot Aussie accent purred from the receiver.

"Um, hey, is this Diego?" *Who else would it be, moron?*

"That's right. Who's this?"

"Gin . . . Ginny Bombay. We met at Borders, remember?"

A warm, luscious laugh filled my right ear. "Of course! I don't easily forget a woman who salts her latte."

I laughed nervously. "Well, I was calling

to take you up on your offer for dinner. If it still stands, that is."

"I'd like that!" He sounded sincere, and my naughty bits became warm and tingly. "How about tonight?"

"Um, sure! Where can I meet you?" It wouldn't do for him to see my assassin's lair. Not on the first date, anyway.

"How about Antonio's at seven?"

Italian food? Did he know that was the way to my bed . . . I mean heart? "Great. See you then."

I hung up and immediately dialed Liv.

"Sure, I'll babysit for Romi and Poppy! I love dogs!" she effused.

"So why don't you have one?" I thought Dak's question was fair, even though he didn't have so much as a houseplant.

"I don't know," she said thoughtfully. "It just seemed like too much of a responsibility."

Obviously I wasn't the only one who felt that way. "Well, enjoy your time with Poppy, then. Maybe she'll change your mind. I'll drop them off at six thirty."

"Great. See you later," Liv said before hanging up.

Okay. Dak had said I needed to relax. And that's what I would do tonight. Relax while mentally undressing Diego. Actually, I wasn't going to wait to do that. My imagination was just getting to the part where I tear off his boxers with my teeth, when I saw Poppy squatting on the carpet. And it wasn't because she was doing lunges. Terrific.

CHAPTER SIX

"Murder is always a mistake. One should never do anything that one cannot talk about after dinner."
—Oscar Wilde

It was kind of funny. I mean, I'd killed lots of men. Some of them had been really scary, intimidating types. And yet, here I was, at Antonio's, waiting for Diego and I was terrified. I guess it had just been a long time since I'd had a real date. And by real, I meant a date that could end up with me and a man naked in a bedroom.

Anyway, he wasn't late; I was early. Which I know you aren't supposed to do. I was supposed to show up after him, making a clothes-melting entrance. Instead, I was early. Damn my training! Mom always said, "Never arrive late for a job. Or you give opportunity to your victim." Was I thinking of Diego as a victim? That made me sound a bit predatory, didn't it?

At least I looked okay . . . I thought. In trying to give the appearance that I could casually throw anything on and walk out the door, I tried on seven different outfits. Two hours later, I settled on dark blue wide-legged dress jeans, a red V-neck cashmere sweater with a white camisole, and my Prada kitten heels. Now all I had to do was stop sweating, not wet myself and somehow keep my heart from bursting out of my chest a la *Alien*.

"You want anything to drink while you wait?" The waiter stood in front of me expectantly. Great. He managed to point out that I was alone, which in food server speak meant "loser."

"Um, how abut a glass of shiraz?" I managed weakly. *Way to project those killer instincts.*

The waiter nodded and left. I looked at my watch. Again. Not much had changed since the last time I checked. So I concentrated on behaving normally. By the way, that wasn't as easy as it sounds. Remember the latte dilemma at the book store?

"You look fantastic." Diego pulled out his chair and joined me.

"Thanks," I replied. "You do too." *Breathe Gin, breathe. No need to be nervous. After all, you've killed men for doing less than dating you.*

The waiter appeared with my wine, and Diego ordered a beer. Now we actually had to come up with something to say.

He really did look amazing. A simple shirt, opened to the third button, blazed brilliant white against his bronzed skin. A black blazer and khaki chinos just looked perfect on his body.

"Come here often?" he asked.

"Oh, yeah. I like this place."

"My first time." He leaned back in his chair and smiled. "I haven't been in town long enough to try everything."

Did I just imagine it, or was he implying that I was one of the things he should try?

"Did you just move here?"

"Temporarily," he answered. "I'm in town for a couple of months with a client. The company's headquarters are located here, and he's been reassigned to the area for about six months."

He could leave me in six months? I began to mourn for a relationship that hadn't even begun yet.

"I see," I said sagely. At least, I hoped it sounded like sage wisdom. With me, you could never tell. "Then where will you go?"

Diego put down his beer. "Probably back to Europe. That's where he was stationed before."

Already, in my mind, I had married Diego, only to lose him to Belgium! "Have you ever been to the Midwest before?"

Diego laughed. "No. This is my first time."

Oooh, the conversation was scintillating, wasn't it? "What do you think?"

"Not bad. I must say that I find the natives intriguing."

"I'll give you the tour sometime." *Ending in my bedroom, of course.*

I had to get it together, but it wasn't easy. In my mind, Diego wasn't human, but a gorgeous fantasy. We scanned the menus and ordered dinner. The waiter left us with bread, extra-virgin olive oil and parmesan cheese. I thought about using the olive oil on Diego.

"So, Ginny, why do you live here?"

Huh? Was that a slam? "I like it here. It's quiet, there are four seasons, and most of my family lives here." I might have sounded a tad defensive.

Diego held up his hands and laughed. "I didn't mean anything by it. Just curious. Most executive protection specialists live in New York, D.C. or L.A."

Oh riiiiiight. The bodyguard cover.

"We have an airport. And my client only works a couple of months a year. So I can live wherever, really. Besides, you live here now. And I don't recall you mentioning living in New York, D.C. or L.A."

Diego nodded. "True." He changed the subject. "So tell me about your family. You're not married—" he pointed to my hand "—at least, I don't think you are."

"I'm widowed, actually."

"My condolences," he said with concern. "I hope I didn't upset you by asking."

"It's all right. Ed died a couple of years ago . . . cancer. I have a little girl who's five. My parents, brother and some of my cousins live here too." I watched him carefully to see if my having a kid bothered him. This date could be over pretty quickly. Hunk be damned, I couldn't tolerate a man who didn't love kids.

I looked into his eyes, and he didn't race out of the restaurant when I mentioned Romi.

"If your daughter is anything like you, I imagine she's quite delightful." Diego smiled, completely relaxed. I took it as a good sign. Make that a very good sign.

"She's wonderful. Funny, smart and independent. I couldn't live without her." Okay, now I was spending too much time talking about it. He might think that I was one of those freaks who lives vicariously through her children.

"I'd very much like to meet her," he said. And I adored him for that.

"Another time, maybe." I needed to change the subject and fast. "So tell me about you." *Nice save.*

"Not much to tell, really. Grew up in Sydney, went to university there, and moved here. There aren't a lot of opportunities in our field in Australia. A friend of mine told me there were jobs here in the States, so I moved here ten years ago and have been in and out of your hemisphere ever since." *Ooooh! He said "in and out"!*

"Do you ever go home?" I couldn't imagine being away from my family. They were pretty cool. Violent, sure, but whose family wasn't dysfunctional?

Diego ran his fingers through his dark wavy hair and I started to melt. "Oh yeah. Sure. I go back a couple of times a year to see Mum and Frida. Dad passed away a while back, and Sis has a couple of kids now. I'm crazy about my niece and nephews."

So he loved kids! And his family! I did a lewd end-zone dance in my mind.

"Well, I'm glad you're here. I don't know anyone to talk about the murders of famous people with."

He laughed, by God, and I went all woozy inside. "Right! By the way, I went back and picked up *Assassination Vacation*. You're right. It is funny."

"Well, maybe we could trace her steps someday and have our own assassination vacation." I choked on my wine—or, more accurately, my words. What the hell was I doing making vacation plans with him?

"I'd like that," he said.

The food arrived, giving me a few minutes to think as I crammed a forkful of pasta into my mouth. For some reason, I didn't feel that the date was going very well. On the one hand, he was still as gorgeous as I remembered, and he liked kids. On the other hand, I felt like a complete idiot. And that's never good, according to those quizzes in *Cosmo*.

"This lasagna is great," Diego said. "I haven't had Italian this good since Venice last year."

"So your client travels a lot?" I managed while twirling my fettuccini onto my fork. He was right. The food was excellent. I could survive on the bread alone. And you could stand a fork up in the alfredo sauce, it was so thick. After all, who needs arteries?

"Yes." He paused to take a sip of his beer before continuing, "When he was stationed in Europe, we went everywhere."

"Do you miss that here?"

"Not at all. I'd like to see more of America sometime. But that will have to wait until I retire. I don't have much time of my own." He dug his fork into his dinner. "Fortunately, my client doesn't need me at night back here."

Don't blow it! Don't blow it! "Good. Then I'll take you out to dinner more often." Had I really said that? Wasn't he supposed to ask for a second date? I did the Jonny Quest "Aaayyiiiiiii" scream in my head.

Diego grinned. "I'd like that, Ginny."

We must have stayed at Antonio's for three hours. I couldn't remember having so much fun with someone other than Ed. Diego was charming, smart and funny. It was like he had stepped out of a book. No man could possibly be this perfect.

"Ginny?" I froze. Uh-oh. I knew that voice.

"Ginny!" Mom said even louder.

I looked up. There they were. My parents.

"Mom! Dad! What're you doing here?" I said with genuine surprise. *Please don't embarrass me*, I prayed silently.

Carolina Bombay drew herself up to her full height of five feet, one inch, and looked from me to Diego. "I didn't know you were seeing someone!"

My prayers didn't work. I guess there really is no God. I looked frantically to my father for support. Dad winked at me and extended his hand. "Larry Bombay, Gin's dad. Please ignore my wife. I'm working to have her institutionalized."

Diego laughed as Mom glared at Dad. Then she turned and offered Diego her hand. "I'm Ginny's mom, Carolina."

"Diego Jones. It's a pleasure to meet you both." I saw my mother's eyebrows go up when she heard the accent.

I would have intervened, but I was completely paralyzed by humiliation. You know, I always thought that if there were a way to kill someone with shame, it would be very effective. *Mental note—give that idea some thought some other time.*

"Mom, Dad, what are you doing here?" I repeated with a little force.

"Oh!" Mom looked back at me. "Sorry. We were shopping and decided to get some dinner." She reached into her bag and pulled something out. "Look what I found for you!"

You know what? It *was* possible to die of shame. I was pretty sure my heart stopped beating at the sight of what was in her hand. I may have been thirty-nine, but for years my mother had been under the delusion that I was ten years old. She had a habit of picking up the goofiest junk at whatever branch of Hell's Mall she shops. This happened several times a year. Usually it was crap shaped like the state of Virginia, mostly with my name on it. Other times it was stationery with kittens and my name on it. But now, my mother held out a pair of barrettes with pugs on them and the name "Ginny" written in puffy paint. Dak had probably called her the minute we left the pet store. Bastard.

I was no psychologist, but I was fairly certain that Mom did this to pretend I was still her innocent baby, in spite of what I did for a living. No excuse. Not this time.

Diego looked at the barrettes, then at

me, his right eyebrow arched in what I hoped was amusement.

"Um, thanks, Mom." I grabbed the barrettes and shoved them in my purse. For some reason, I could never throw this stuff away. It occupied a dusty box in the darkest corner of my attic. The only thing she had ever given me that I did use was a coffee mug that said *Virginia Is for Lovers*. I really liked that.

At the moment, I was pretty sure I looked shell-shocked. Dad gave me a look, then grabbed Mom by the arm.

"Come on, honey, we should get a table."

"Maybe we could join them?" She pointed at the two other chairs.

My eyes flew wide open, and I sent my father the following message, telepathically, *Get her out of here before I tell Diego I'm adopted!* Dad immediately dragged Mom away.

"Oh my God, Diego! I'm so sorry." I could feel the blush all over my face.

Diego waved it off. "No worries. Remember my sister? Mum doesn't even have to be around to embarrass her. All anyone has to do is ask her for her name."

In spite of his sincerity, I was still shaken from the great barrette incident. I mean, did she really think I'd wear them? I had short hair, for Christ's sake! Really short hair!

Diego leaned closer. "Gin, really, don't fret about it. Okay?"

I nodded. "Okay." But I was convinced Mom had blown my chances of getting to second base with Diego tonight.

We would've stayed longer, but the waiter forced us out. I considered killing him for ending my date before I could reduce the damage Mom had done. But it wouldn't do to murder someone in front of my future husband.

Diego walked me to my car. He was just starting to make his move and kiss me when he froze, a frown crossing his lickable features. He reached for his belt, pulling out a cell phone.

"Damn," he said quietly. "It's my client. I have to take this." Diego looked at me as if to see if that was okay. I nodded, and he answered his phone.

I could've heard what he said, but I was easily hypnotized by his eyes, which were on mine in spite of his conversation. He had this dark, hungry look. I recognized that. That was a good look! As soon as he snapped off the phone, I reached up and kissed him.

Diego kissed back. *Yaaaaaayyyyyy!* His lips were soft, needy. He tasted like the mint he'd gotten from the waiter. Diego pulled me to him, his lips against mine. I seriously considered swooning.

"I've got to go," he said quietly, his forehead against mine. "I'll call you tomorrow, and we'll make plans, okay?"

I nodded like a puppet. His kiss totally threw my mojo off. He waited until I got in the car and drove away. I only hoped that in my blissed-out, aroused state I wouldn't drive into a house on the way home.

CHAPTER SEVEN

John Smith: "What's new?" Eddie:
"Same old, same old. People need
killing."

—Mr. & Mrs. Smith

"All right, we want details!" Liv and Dak
faced me with their arms crossed. I had
just gotten back from taking Romi to
school and found them on my doorstep.
Apparently, Liv had told Dak about my
date last night. Assassins are such nosy
bastards.

"Why didn't you tell me you had a
date?" Dak asked.

"Because I made the decision to call
him after you left."

"Well?" Liv asked. "Who is he?" She
enunciated each word as if I were three
years old.

I sighed and took another drink of my
coffee. I had a mild headache from the
two bottles of wine I had consumed. "His
name is Diego. He's Australian. I met him
at the bookstore."

"Ooooh! A man with an accent!" Liv squealed.

Dak rolled his eyes. "And?"

I shrugged. "What?" I knew I was pissing him off, and it amused me.

Dak sighed with frustration. "Details! I want details!"

I pointed at him. "Do I ever ask you for details of your dates?"

"No. But they don't seem to be as important to me as this guy is to you."

I arched my right eyebrow. "How can you tell?"

Dak counted on his fingers. "One, you haven't dated since Eddie died. Two, Liv said you were out for four hours . . . on a weeknight. And three, you're hiding something."

It was my turn to roll my eyes. "You're an idiot. I'm not hiding anything. I'm just not telling you everything."

"And there's a difference?" Dak asked.

"Yeah, there is."

"Do I have to put you both in time-out?" Liv pushed us apart. She turned to me. "We're just curious. And we're happy for you. That's all, Gin."

Liv knew which buttons to push. But I was afraid to tell them too much. It wasn't real yet. At least not to me.

"What do you want to know?" I offered my olive branch.

"How about his name, Social Security

number and mother's maiden name?"
Dak asked.

"Right. Like I'd let you do a background
check on him." And he would too.

"How about just a little info?" Liv asked
gently.

"Okay. He's probably our age, gorgeous
as all get out in that tall-dark-handsome
kind of way. He's very funny and smart
and likes kids. Happy?"

"What does he do for a living?" Dak
asked.

And there it was. The thing I didn't
want to tell them. Why? Because there
was a teensy, weensy chance that there
could be, in the way distant future, a
slight conflict of interest there.

"He's a bodyguard." I couldn't lie to
them. Dak and Liv knew me too well.

"A what? Gin! Are you crazy?" Dak
jumped in.

"Now, Dak, we don't know that it'll be a
problem," Liv said.

Dak rolled his eyes. "Oh, sure. Won't be
a problem! He just happens to be a bodyguard in a small city where my immediate
family of assassins lives! I'm sure there
won't be any conflict of interest there."
Wow. He was pissed!

"I didn't know that when I met him! It's
just what he does. It's not like he's FBI or
a cop."

Okay, I'd admit to that one time I'd had

a date with a Fed by mistake. But it had never come back to haunt me, and there'd been no second date. (Relax. I didn't kill him.)

"At least she had a date!" Liv interjected.

I threw my hands up in the air. "Now, that doesn't make me sound pathetic at all!"

Poppy padded into the room and looked at us. Apparently we'd woken her up. Finding nothing interesting, she waddled to her food dish and began eating.

"See what you did? You woke the baby!" I yelled at Dak.

Dak waved his hands in the air. "Okay, fine. I'm overreacting. I'm glad you're seeing someone. Even if he is body armor." Body armor was what we called bodyguards. They usually slowed the process of hitting our target with bullets.

"I accept your apology," I said rather magnanimously.

"So." Liv popped a Hostess mini-muffin in her mouth. (The girl never, ever gained weight.) "Are you going to see him again?"

"Did you get laid?" Dak cut in.

I threw my hands into the air. "Yes," I said to Liv. Then I turned to Dak. "Not yet, not that it's any of your business. Besides, he's only here for six months, then it's back to Europe with his client. I can't imagine us having a long-distance thing after—goddamnit! It's only been one date! Why am I telling you all this?"

Liv looked to Dak. "She's a little defensive, isn't she?"

"No shit," he responded. "She needs to get laid."

"I'm right *here!*" I shouted. I hated being ignored. "And there's nothing to discuss!"

I scooped up the fat pug puppy, walked out the back door, and set Poppy down in the yard. I followed her while she used my lawn as her personal toilet, then brought her back in. Liv and Dak were waiting for me.

"Okay, we'll change the subject." Dak smiled. "What's the job?"

I blinked at him. "What are you talking about?"

"The job! Who's Vic?"

"What?" I had no clue.

Dak stared at me. "The envelope I gave you yesterday! Who's Vic?"

"Oh." I'd forgotten about that. Vic was the name we gave our victims, kind of like a secret code. Not the most difficult code to crack, but we're kind of lazy. "I didn't open it." I had forgotten about the hit. I'd been too wrapped up in Diego's eyes—I mean, Romi's (and Poppy's) training.

"I'll open it later." We had a couple of weeks. And I needed to focus on other things first.

"You have to do it before the reunion," Dak pressed.

"I know." I scratched between Poppy's ears. "I'll get to it. When have you ever known me to screw up a job?"

"Never," Dak mused, "but there's a first time for everything."

"Out." I pointed to the door.

Liv fondled the pug's ears, then smiled as she grabbed Dak by the arm and pulled him out of my house.

"Now, you, I like," I said in a baby voice to Poppy. She wiggled in my arms. "You don't ask any questions." I set her on the floor and walked into the living room. The pup trailed me, trying clumsily to climb onto the couch next to me. I lifted her up, and she snuggled onto my lap, promptly falling asleep.

The envelope sat on the end table, unopened. I supposed I shouldn't leave it there, but I was getting careless these days. I picked it up and turned it around in my hands, giving myself one nasty paper cut.

"That's enough for you," I said as I set it down and sucked on my finger. There was a lot to think about. A hit that had to be taken care of, the family reunion, training Romi, housetraining Poppy, and an impending second date with the delectable Diego.

I thought about the kiss he had given me last night. It had been perfect in every way. I wanted more. When would he call? Oh yes, he had said today sometime.

Now, assassins don't usually sit by the phone waiting for Australian bodyguards to call them for a date. Okay, so I was breaking that rule. I knew there would be a second date, followed by a third, fourth, all the way to 100 if I could make it happen. How many days are there in six months? Something like 180 to 186, I would imagine. Minus the reunion time and, of course, I'd be working some of the time too. Hmmm . . . this relationship had to move fast in order for first date plus consecutive dates to equal mind-blowing sex.

Okay, so I'd break with convention and wait by the phone today. Poppy snored loudly on my lap. It wasn't like I could move anyway.

And that's where I sat for four hours, waiting for the phone to ring and my bladder to explode. Funny business, this dating thing. Finally, I had to get up to pick up Romi from school. Diego hadn't called. Bastard.

CHAPTER EIGHT

Mr. Newberry: "I visualized you in a haze as one of those slackster, flannel-wearing, coffee-house misanthropes I've been seeing in Newsweek."

Marty: "No no no, I went the other road. Six figures, doing business with lead pipe cruelty, mercenary sensibility. You know . . . sports, sex, no real relationships. How about you—how have the years been treating you?"

Mr. Newberry: "Well you know me, Martin—still the same old sellout, exploiting the oppressed . . ."

—Grosse Pointe Blank

I'd spent all day waiting for Diego to call. And I hadn't given up yet, as evidenced by the cordless phone sitting next to me. However, Dak had been right. I had a job to do and that monkey would be on my back until I did it.

Now, with Romi in bed and Poppy curled up with her, I had some time to check out the hit. It was just an ordinary manila envelope, nothing special, no scary seal in bloodred wax. You weren't expecting that, right?

Jobs were handed down through the

family, assigned by the Council to the assassin, based on location, specialty, and so on. The Council consisted of the oldest Bombay generation, which in this case was Grandma Mary, her brother Lou, sister Dela (as in Delaware) and cousins Troy and Florence, who headed up the European branch of the Bombays. You might think that sounds efficient to have American and European branches. But basically it goes back 150 years when only part of the family wanted to come to America. The other snobs refused to leave The Continent.

It was useful to have us working internationally. And I got along well with my European counterparts. It also gave me a place to crash when in England or France. Anyway, the Council met quarterly, handing down assignments to their children (Mom's generation), who were divided into subsets with Greek letter codes—a tradition going back to our Greek heritage. Mom was the head of the Alpha group, the group to which Dak and I belonged. Liv and her brother, Paris, were in the Beta subset. Mom's sister, Virginia, hadn't lived long enough to have kids, so she had zip. It was a small but lethal family. I wouldn't cross us.

So I sat in the living room with the drapes drawn and security system on. Technically, I should have been in the lab to do this, but I was feeling pretty lazy. That's right, I was a lazy assassin.

"Let's see who our bad guy is today, Gin!" I announced in my game-show voice to no one in particular. (Insert embarrassed assassin here.)

Leonard Burns's forgettable face glowered at me. Soon, it would be a dead face, if I had anything to do with it. Let's see, busted for selling military secrets to Iran. *Who's been a bad boy? You have, you have!*

Apparently, Leonard, now to be referred to as "Vic," had turned federal witness and got away with screwing over his country. For some reason, Leonard cheated death through the federal witness protection program by hiding out in my backyard. It took a while to find him, but Grandma had tracked him down. *Mental note: appreciate Grandma more. Maybe send a card or flowers—just because.*

Hmmm, currently employed with our local farm implement manufacturer as an engineer. Nice. Didn't live far from me either, only two blocks away.

So the next morning, after taking Romi to school, I set my evil (dun, dun, dun!) plan in motion.

"Come on, Poppy," I said cheerfully as I wrestled her into a harness, "we're going for a walk!" By the way, have you ever tried to put one of those things on a dog? I swear they were designed by the sadist who came up with the straightjacket. And if you've ever had to put a straightjacket on someone, you know what I mean. If you haven't, um, well, just take my word for it.

It was a gorgeous day for surveillance work. With the memorized address, my mirrored aviator sunglasses and baseball cap (I had other clothes on too), I'd look like anyone else taking a two-month-old pug for a walk. Poppy bounced beside me, seemingly happy with this particular interruption in her intensive napping schedule.

It only took a few minutes to find Vic's house—without looking like I was trying to find his house, that is. It was probably not called a house as much as a palace.

In fact, I hadn't realized I lived in such a nice neighborhood. The large, brick neoclassical monstrosity loomed three stories above me. Four fluted columns rose in front of the entrance to the top floor. The trim was oddly eclectic. How did you hide out in something that begged for attention?

Okay, I had to check the grounds. If he had a garden, I might get lucky and find rhubarb or rhododendron to poison him with and make it look like Li'l Ol' Leo just had an accidental hankerin' to eat from his garden. But how did I explain snooping around?

A whimper at my feet gave me an idea. I

bent down to scratch Poppy, surreptitiously unhooking her leash. There was no better excuse than chasing a runaway puppy.

There was one problem with that, however. I hadn't factored in the complete lack of interest my dog had in doing anything more than sitting on the sidewalk.

"Go, Poppy! Go on, girl!" I whispered, nudging her gently with my foot. She lay down.

"Come on!" I whispered a little loudly. "This is your big chance! Make a break for it!" Poppy lifted her head to stare at me, eyes bulging, lips permanently etched in a sour look. She sneezed, then wiggled her curled-up tail.

Maybe I was getting somewhere. "That's it! Go on! Check out the house! Look at those bushes! I'll bet there's a dead bird or something just as gross over there!"

Poppy rose to her feet, then yawned while stretching her front legs. I was impressed. I'd never seen her do more than one thing at a time before. She remained standing, looking to me for more encouragement.

"Good girl!" I said as she finally waddled off toward the house. We would need to work on that. I wondered if there was a *dis*obedience class I could take. While Poppy traveled at speeds that would allow a paralyzed snail to catch her, I pretended to be fascinated by my watch. Out of the corner of my eye, I spotted her lying down beneath a shrub in front of the house. Okay, so not in the backyard, but I could still pull it off.

"Ginny!" Diego's voice called out behind me, and I turned to see him get out of a black town car and walk toward me.

You would be glad to know I didn't panic. I may have vomited a little in my mouth, but no trace of panic. "Diego? What are you doing here?"

"My client lives on this street." He looked at the empty leash in my hands. "Did you lose your dog?"

"What? Oh! Yes! I was just looking for her." To make it appear more realistic, I shouted, "Here Poppy! Poppy! Come here, girl!" I prayed that she wouldn't hear me.

"What a darling pug!" Diego exclaimed as the puppy betrayed me by running up to us. Oh sure, *now* she ran.

Poppy wagged her rear end, no doubt delighted to be fondled by this gorgeous alpha male. Wish I knew what that was like. How pathetic was it that my dog got more action than I did? Before my brain registered what was happening, Diego scooped Poppy up in his arms.

"You're so cute!" The little traitor squirmed with glee. "You say her name's Poppy?"

"Yeah. I just got her." Okay, I'd admit I

was more than a little jealous of my dog. I snapped the leash onto her harness and retrieved her from his arms.

Diego smiled. "Sorry I didn't call earlier. We had a death threat come in yesterday. You know, the usual stuff."

"Oh. No problem. I've been too busy to notice," I lied. Badly.

"So you live around here?" Diego smiled. He saw right through my clothes . . . I mean lies.

"Um, yes. Two blocks away, actually."

Diego squinted into the distance. "I can walk you home."

"No," I may have said a little too quickly. "Poppy hasn't, you know, done what we set out to do." Nice save. I still wanted to get a little surveillance done, and I wasn't ready for him to see my house. My bed, yes. My house, no. Of course, I wasn't exactly sure how to pull that off.

He looked down, then at me with a smile. "Seems she just took care of business."

Damn. Poppy wagged her curly tail as best she could, next to a steaming pile of "business."

So that's how Diego ended up in my kitchen, with a diet pop and a smile. Under normal circumstances, I would have been thrilled. But somehow, it was too soon to have him in my house. Instead of lust, all I felt was weird. And not good weird either, but the walk in on your-father-naked kind of weird.

Diego looked at his watch. "I lost track of the time. Gotta run!" He stood, and I walked him to the door. Before I opened it, he kissed me lightly on the lips. Okay. The weird feeling was replaced with lust again. All circuits were back to normal.

"It was nice meeting you, Poppy." He crouched to pet the wriggling, delighted pug. The whore. Diego stood. "How about I bring a pizza over one night and meet your daughter?"

"Um, okay." I was still a little fogged up over the kiss.

"Tomorrow night all right?" Diego punctuated his question with a more passionate kiss.

"Yeah. Sure," I think I responded.

Diego left and I slumped against the closed door, sliding down to the floor with my new competition for the Australian bodyguard's affections. Poppy licked my hand, then curled up in my lap and promptly fell asleep.

I stroked her ears until she started snoring. "You know, I should pop a cap in your ass. After all, you blew every assignment I gave you today, and then you shamelessly threw yourself at my man."

In her sleepy state, Poppy stretched and rolled over, exposing her fat belly to me, waiting for a scratch.

"I guess it's a good thing I have a policy against killing animals."

Poppy ignored me, clearly getting her beauty sleep so she could seduce my new boyfriend tomorrow night. For a two-month-old puppy, she seemed to have it all figured out.

CHAPTER NINE

"If I show up at your door, chances are you did something to bring me there."
—Martin Blank, *Grosse Pointe Blank*

After a much-needed cold shower and lunch, I plopped Poppy in her crate and headed out for a quick, two-block jog. I figured the neighbors might get suspicious if they saw me again with the puppy, so I altered my "disguise" a bit and left to make it look like a different woman in the throes of exercising.

Maybe I should mention that I hate jogging. I only ever did it once, at Ed's request. He was a runner and wanted me to join him. After one minute, I nearly passed out. I just wasn't cut out for it. I can sprint like an axe-toting maniac in a hockey mask, but I simply can't jog.

Which is why I was completely out of breath when I got to Vic's place (only two blocks away). After passing in front of it, I went around the block, looking for an alley or way to his backyard. No alley. And the foliage was too thick to see the back of the house from the yard behind. So I came around and crossed to the other side of the street, pausing across the street from Vic's mansion.

Pretending to stop and answer my cell phone, I managed to use it to take a few pictures of the front of the house. I'd have to come up with a way to check out the grounds later. Maybe Dak would come over to watch Romi for me so I could do a little recon under the cover of darkness.

The driveway was clear but the garage door was shut. There might be a Mrs. Vic at home, for all I knew. Glancing up and down the street, I tried to find a neighbor I might know. None of the houses or addresses looked familiar. What now?

There is a fine art to assassination. It isn't like the movies where the hit man busts in, guns a-blazing. That just doesn't work in real life. I try to learn as much as possible before I even begin. I know, booooring. What do you expect? This is reality, not some movie.

Back at home, an Internet search yielded some good stuff. Through his company's Web site, I discovered that Vic was in the Chamber of Commerce and the Rotary Club. That made me smile. I enjoyed hitting Rotarians almost as much as I enjoyed waxing Junior Leaguers.

Something about those stupid clubs makes me itch.

On Google, I found out that Vic has no Mrs. Vic and no little Vics. That's good. Oooh! He doesn't give to charity either! Score! I love that! If he gave to the Humane Society or something, that would bother me. Unless he left it in his will. You know, I always thought it would be a good idea for these foundations to set up a contract with us. That way, shortly after naming a charity in their wills, we could pop them. Everybody wins!

Okay, so I had a little information. I still needed to know more personal stuff. I went to my next professional source—the Kennedy Elementary Student Directory. The school district would probably disapprove of the directory's use for this purpose, but Vic lived in the neighborhood, and maybe one of Romi's friends lived nearby. I could pump the parents for info and no one would be the wiser.

I scanned the directory, looking at addresses first. I figured I could come up with just about any excuse to visit a fellow Kennedy parent, even if they had no connection to Romi.

Voila! I found one. And right next door, nonetheless. Yay! Looking at the header, I saw that it was even someone in Romi's class. Bonus!

Damn. The victory was short-lived.

Guess who the neighbor was? That's right. Vivian Marcy. For once in my life, that woman had something I needed. I hoped the gods were whooping it up in Valhalla over that one.

Get over it, Gin. You have a job to do. Hey! Maybe you can find a way to make it look like Vivian killed him! My day just got a little brighter. Now I needed a pretext. Vivian would get suspicious if I just showed up on her doorstep. What I needed was a very good excuse.

"Mommy!" Romi cried as she plowed into me after school.

I chatted with my daughter about her day as we walked back to the car. At home we went through our ritual, snack and backpack review. I pulled out a large envelope.

"What's this?" I asked Romi.

"Oh. We're s'posed to sell stuff. It's for the playground," Romi sputtered through a mouthful of cookies.

Great. School started two weeks ago and already we had to sell junk. I flipped through the booklet: candy, candles, calendars—all the "c" words were there. Was it just my imagination, or did kids have to sell a lot of crap (hey, another "c" word!) these days? The only thing I remembered selling in school was Girl Scout cookies. And I think in high school,

the Future Farmers of America had sold
oranges or something. Last year, Romi's
preschool had peddled junk in the fall
and spring. I didn't want to mess with it,
so I just walked into the office and
handed them a check for $100. It seemed
a lot easier than . . .

That was it! I grabbed the phone and dialed Vivian's number.

"Hello?" Vivian sounded bored. Must be
rough to break up a day of polishing your
Tiffany jewelry by answering the phone.

"Vivian? It's Ginny."

"Who?" said the bored voice again.

I clenched my teeth. She knew damn
well who it was. "Ginny Bombay."

"Oh, Virginia," she responded, with my
full name, just to piss me off. "I've been
meaning to call you."

I dug my fingernails into my palms.
"Really? I want to talk to you too. Are you
free tomorrow morning? I could stop by?"
I cringed at the thought of entering her
home. Maybe I should take some holy water with me, just to be safe.

"Fine," she replied. "I'll see you at ten."
She hung up before I could confirm. I figured I'd better pack a mirror too. Just in
case she was really a gorgon underneath
all that Chanel makeup.

The next morning found me doing something I would never have imagined in a

million years. I was walking to Vivian Marcy's house. And chances were, we would have a cup of coffee. Just the thought of accepting hospitality from that woman made me nervous. I couldn't remember whether she wore any large rings that might conceal poison.

My fingers flew up to the heart-shaped locket around my neck. Inside, behind a photo of my daughter, was my mandatory cyanide pill (death before captivity). Dak kept his in his watch. Liv had hers in her medical-alert bracelet—she was allergic to bee stings.

Vivian's house was almost a complete replica of Tara. I rang the doorbell. It even played the theme song from *Gone with the Wind*. Yeesh. What an ego.

"Come in, Virginia." She stood in the doorway, this time in a pink Juicy Couture jogging suit. I followed her down the hall to a three-season room in the back of the house. It had a perfect view of Vic's yard. Despite being in Vivian's sinister lair, this was a definite bonus.

"Thanks," I said, accepting a cup of coffee from my hostess. "You have a lovely yard." My teeth were clenched, but I believed I sounded sincere.

Vivian waved me off. "Oh it's nothing. My gardener does it. I don't even know what's all out there."

Trying not to appear too eager, I responded, "I was a botany minor in college . . . mind if I look around?" I was out the door before she could stop me.

Damn. It really was a gorgeous spread. Early autumn hadn't yet touched her flowers, and they bloomed brightly against the well-manicured lawn. Vivian walked alongside me, saying nothing as I "oohed" and "ahhhed" over her assortment of lilies, wildflowers and hostas.

From time to time, my eyes crossed over into Vic's yard, but I didn't see any toxic plants. No rhododendron, lily of the valley or black-eyed Susans. Not even a stray mushroom. Obviously, the FBI took its witness protection program seriously.

"Is that an elderberry bush?" I walked toward a shrub filled with berries at the border between Vivian's and Leonard's property. It was! Hmmm . . . maybe I had found something useful after all.

"I don't know," Vivian said tersely. "Let's go back inside. I'm not that fond of the outdoors."

I rolled my eyes and followed her inside. Now I had to make her forget we were ever out there.

"Vivian, I see the PTA has sent home a fundraising brochure."

"Yes, for playground equipment." She sounded bored again.

"Well, there are so many fundraisers

this time of the year, I had an idea for raising money."

"Really?" Her eyes widened, as if she were surprised I was capable of intelligent thought.

I ignored her expression. "I was thinking I'd rather just write a check to the school and be done with it. That way, all the money goes directly to the project, not just a percentage. And there's no work involved with taking orders, delivering orders and collecting money."

"Good for you. But how does that help?" I could see she didn't think I had an idea.

"If I would rather do that, my guess is other parents would rather do that too. The school could make a lot more money and the parents would be happy they didn't have to sell junk to everyone they know."

Vivian leaned back and took a sip of her coffee. She was frowning, which probably meant that she was pissed she hadn't come up with the idea herself. Even though this idea was just a pretext to scope Vic's yard, I thought it had real merit. I didn't need any pumpkin spice candles or tins full of cashews any more than the next guy.

"I like that," Vivian responded with a frown. Only she could make a good idea feel bad. "Of course, we've already started the fundraiser, but maybe I could turn your little idea"—she waved her hand at me, dismissively—"into a real, workable project for the spring."

I suppressed a rising tide of fury. It didn't matter what she thought, or that she was planning to put her name on it and reap the glory. I had done what I wanted to do. Vivian would do everything she could to forget I even stopped by so she could claim the idea as her own. Mission accomplished.

"Now, Virginia, there is something I wanted to talk to you about as well."

I'm pretty sure my expression registered fear and surprise. "What?"

"I want you to start a Daisy troop for the kindergarten class." She looked like Cleopatra handing down an edict. I wished I had an asp handy, but they're not native to this area.

"I don't have time for that. . . . I don't even know what that is!" I protested.

Vivian continued, "I'm sure you don't. In our day, we started Girl Scouts with Brownies. Now, it starts with Daisy Scouts in kindergarten. It's very easy. Even you can do this."

For a moment, I thought about holding her down and shoving handfuls of raw elderberries down her throat. It would take quite a few, but it would be worth it to watch her go through the stages of dizziness, headache, nausea, vomiting, gastroenteritis, respiratory difficulty, convulsions, and if I was really lucky, death. I imagined sitting there, calmly, drinking my coffee and watching her body convulse on the floor. Of course, I'd wipe everything down before leaving. Because she was completely ignorant of what was in her backyard, the coroner would probably rule the death accidental.

"You're not listening to me, Virginia!" she snapped.

"Oh, sorry," I said. *I'm just imagining your painful death.*

"Look, it's very simple. You aren't allowed to go camping or sell cookies. Just have a meeting or two each month."

"I don't think so, Vivian. I've got a lot on my plate right now. . . ."

She raised her hand to silence me. "It's very easy. Romi can even join."

Again, I fought back the urge to race to her backyard with a bowl to begin collecting berries. "What do you mean by that?"

"I don't mean anything by it. Really, Virginia. You are so touchy." She handed me a piece of paper with a list of names and dates for training. "Call Sarah Wendt. I'll let the three kindergarten teachers know you're recruiting."

Before I knew it, I was standing on the

other side of her closed front door, hold-ing a piece of paper and wondering what happened.

I had barely made it home when the phone rang. The caller ID said it was none other than Sarah Wendt.

"Hi, Ginny! I'm so glad you're going to lead our troop!" The bubbly blonde on the other end of the line started before I could say so much as "hello."

"But Sarah, I don't know anything about running a Girl Scout troop! I didn't even tell Vivian I would do it!"

"No problem. I scheduled your troop for a meeting next week. You're gonna love it! See you Wednesday!" She hung up before I could answer.

"Okay," I said to Liv ten minutes later in my kitchen, "all I wanted to do was get a look at Vic's yard. Now I'm leading a Daisy Scout troop?"

Liv laughed. "You've done some bizarre things before, Gin. But I think this is my favorite."

Only Liv could get away with that. "I guess I should've expected that when I went over there, huh?"

Liv nodded. "Duh! You delivered your-self into her evil clutches. Willingly, I might add."

"Now my to-do list is really fucked up. How am I going to pull it all together? The reunion, Diego, Romi's training, the job,

cookies shaped like whatever and now
starting a Girl Scout troop?"

"Maybe you could make witch cookies
that resemble Vivian?" Liv suggested.

Hmmm . . . not a bad idea. "I'm serious!"

"Okay," Liv began, "I'll help you with
the troop. I'd like to get Alta into scouting
anyway. We can do the training together
and be co-leaders. It'll be a way to spend
time with the girls."

I rubbed my chin. "Maybe. I don't know."

Liv continued, "And I'll help with the
job, and we'll train the girls together.
We'll be together at the reunion too. The
only thing I can't help you with is your
sex life. I have to draw the line there."

"I don't think you should rule it out," I
teased. "You'd like him. He's really hot."

She shook her head. "No threesomes.
That's my policy."

"I'll bet Todd hates that," I murmured.

"Do you feel better about this?" Liv
asked, ignoring my comment.

I nodded, "Well, yeah, since you're holding my hand on everything else."

She stayed for a couple of hours and we
reviewed the file I had started on Vic.
When Liv left, she told me she would try
to find out more about him.

As I put the dishes in the dishwasher, I
realized that even with Liv's help, I was in
way over my head. As if that were a first
for me.

CHAPTER TEN

"It's not that I'm afraid to die; I just don't want to be there when it happens."

—Woody Allen

I stood in the doorway, my mouth hanging open. Which, by the way, was not a good look for me.

Diego grinned, a large pizza in his hands. "Hope you like pepperoni."

I nodded. "It's my favorite. How did you know?"

"You just struck me as a pepperoni type."

"Really?" I asked, wondering what made me seem like a long, hard, red Italian salami.

"No. I just called Pizza Hut and asked what you usually get."

"They tell you that?" Hmmm, that might be a useful tool in the future. Maybe I could get poisonous mushrooms on a Vic's pizza.

Diego nodded. "Hard to believe, I know.

I'll have to make sure my client doesn't use Pizza Hut."

Damn, there went my brilliant idea.

"Gin?" Diego's smoky voice slid into my thoughts. "Can I come in?"

"Oh! Yeah!" I stumbled backward to let him in.

"Mommy?" Romi appeared as soon as I closed the door behind Diego.

"Honey," I replied, "this is my friend Diego."

Diego knelt down to make eye contact. "You must be Romi. I've heard a lot about you. And you are just as lovely as your mum said."

I'd like to note that if we were playing "strip date," I would have already removed my pants.

"Okay," Romi responded, "you can be my friend too." Good girl.

I watched in amazement as Diego and Romi charmed each other throughout dinner. She listened to every word he said, and he acted as though she was the only person in the world. I just sat there like a lump, with a goofy smile pasted on my face.

"Mommy hasn't had a boyfriend before. Not since Dad died, I think."

I froze in my seat, smile fading rapidly. "Romi!"

Diego shook his head. "It's all right, really."

"How about some ice cream?" I said, jumping to my feet.

"Yay!" Romi cried out.

In just a few minutes, I had managed to keep her little, overactive mouth busy with three scoops of chocolate ice cream. Maybe three scoops was a little excessive, but I had to make sure she wouldn't say anything like that again. Maybe I should have thrown in some gooey marshmallow topping.

I wasn't angry with her, just a little embarrassed. But why should I be? It was the truth. Being a widow was nothing to be ashamed of. I mean, it's not like *I* killed him.

"She's a great kid," Diego whispered as we shut the door to her bedroom. Okay, so I used her little comment to impose a slightly early bedtime. She can't tell time yet.

"Thanks. She comes from good breeding stock." *Yikes!* I could not believe I said that. Trying to make him forget I had hinted at sex, I settled us on the couch in the family room with a bottle of red wine.

"You're pretty fantastic with kids," I said.

"I love them. I think I told you about my niece and nephews on our last date."

"Oh, so this is a date?"

Diego grinned, winning my shirt in the aforementioned imaginary strip game. "That's what I thought."

I smiled smugly as he put his arm around me. Damn, he smelled good. It had been so long since a gorgeous man touched me—without fighting for his life, that is.

"Okay," I replied, "if this is a date, I expect you to tell me more about yourself."

Diego squeezed me gently. "What exactly do you want to know?"

"Well," I responded, leaning against him, "I guess I should know the usual stuff—what trips your trigger . . . do I trip your trigger? . . . that kind of thing."

"Ah. Well, I can answer the second question first. You do. I think you are the most unusual woman I've ever met."

"Uh, is that good or bad? 'Cause I can see it taken either way."

"Unusual is good. In your case, very, very good."

I was blushing. So I changed the subject slightly (I don't want to lose that train of thought just yet). "How about the first question?"

Diego's fingers started to stroke my shoulder, and I was afraid of losing consciousness. "I like piña coladas. And getting caught in the rain. I'm not much into health food . . ."

"Okay," I protested, "you're not gonna cough it up. Fine."

Diego laughed, "Actually, that's not too far off. I'm a pretty easygoing guy. I like all kinds of food, have no favorite color, and while I enjoy virtually every kind of music, I prefer jazz and Spanish guitar."

I raised my eyebrows. "That's pretty specific."

"And you?"

"I'm kind of the same. I love Italian food, everything but rap in the music area, orange is my favorite color, and you trip my trigger too."

Diego leaned in and kissed me. That shut me up. Oh my God did he have wonderful lips! Every movement felt like a caress, and my lips pulsed in time to my flamenco heartbeat. After a few moments, he pulled back. As he looked into my eyes, I realized that this conversation was over. Before I could figure out if it was wise to do this without making sure Romi was passed out, I pulled his lips to mine and kissed him ferociously.

Diego moaned and the sound did all sorts of naughty things to me. His voice was so raw, so warm, I couldn't focus on anything more than the moment. My living room dissolved around me and the only thing in the universe was Diego's lips on mine.

He gently parted my lips with his tongue, slipping in slightly to stroke my mouth. I moaned deeply and Diego pulled me onto his lap.

I don't know how long we kissed, maybe hours, maybe weeks. At first I wanted to get right to the meat of the sex, but then I realized that I'd never kissed anyone like this before. It was amazing. Sensual. Liberating. Wait, *liberating?* What the hell did that mean?

"Gin?" Diego had pulled away and was staring at me. "Are you okay?"

"Um, sure. Why?" Hormones fogged my brain. What did I do?

"You weren't breathing."

"Oh. Right. I'll remember that," I said, pressing my lips to his again.

A voice spoke up, and I responded, "I'm breathing! Trust me, air is going in and out of my lungs."

Laughter followed. Shit. I recognized that voice.

"Dak!" I scrambled off Diego's lap. "What the hell are you doing here?"

Dak grinned, his whole face lighting up with amusement, "Just checking on you. You said you wanted me to watch Romi while you did some work."

I did ask my dumb-ass brother to babysit. But tomorrow night! Not tonight!

Diego rose from the sofa and extended his right hand cautiously. "Diego Jones. And you are?"

Dak responded with reserve. "Dakota, Gin's brother." Why do men have to act so weird all the time?

Diego relaxed and smiled. I, on the other hand, glared at my brother.

"Dak, that was for tomorrow night. Not tonight."

He slapped his forehead. "Oh, right. Sorry about that." Then the bastard took a seat. I toyed with the idea of poisoning him. No, that would just piss Mom off.

"Out!" I found my voice. "Or I'll kill you." Okay, so I was only half kidding.

Dak held up his hands. "All right, fine. Tomorrow night it is." He turned to Diego. "It was nice meeting you." Diego responded the same way and my asshole brother left.

"He seems okay," Diego mused. "I think I've met everyone now."

That was sad but true. Once again, my family had invaded my personal space. From my neurotic mother and good-natured father to my bastard brother, Diego had met them all within the same week I met him. Oy vey.

"I'm sorry. He's just a little . . ." I couldn't think of the appropriate adjective. "I guess my family had me followed."

"It's fine, really. In fact, I think it's rather nice."

I arched my right eyebrow. "Really?"

Diego laughed. "Really. Charming actually."

"Charming? Are you insane? This is the kind of stuff that usually drives men away! A single mother approaching forty, whose mother acts like she's twelve, whose brother stalks her on dates? Do you go out with women like me a lot?"

"No," he said with a smile. "It's just nice to see a family who is so close. My father died when I was at university. And Mum is, well, colorful."

Oooh! I'd forgotten his father was dead. I wanted to comfort him. Something about being an orphan screamed, *Let me make it all go away.*

"Sorry about that. Your father, I mean."

"It's okay. I just learned to appreciate family more, that's all."

Okay, now he had my underwear. If only this game of strip date were real. . . .

Poppy padded into the room, sniffing the floor and indicating that she wanted to go outside.

"I have to take her out," I said to Diego. "I'll be right back." *Oh, and feel free to remove any constrictive articles of clothing while I'm gone.*

Once outside, I took a deep breath. Poppy waddled around the yard, looking for the perfect spot to kill my grass. This thing with Diego was going fast. Not that I minded. I wasn't exactly the pillar of moral turpitude, myself. Mentally, I had convinced myself this was just a fling. Why not just have sex and move on?

Wow. I hadn't even had sex for a while. What if I did something wrong? How could you do something wrong? It was pretty simple, really, stick-plug-into-socket technology at best.

Obviously the attraction was there. Was it ever! And I was pretty sure he wanted me too. Okay! That's it! I'm gonna go in there and have mind-altering sex!

I walked confidently into the kitchen, announcing triumphantly, "I'm ready!" Then my jaw went slack. Diego was putting on his coat! Why in the hell was he doing that?

"Sorry, Gin." He had the grace to look a little crushed. "My client just got a suspicious phone call. I have to check it out."

"What?" *What*? How could this happen? I was ready, dammit!

Diego kissed me on the lips. "At least you're in the business and know what I'm dealing with. Most women wouldn't be so understanding."

"Oh sure, I understand," I said weakly. Okay, so I didn't mean it. But what could I do? I'd told him I was a bodyguard. It was my own damn fault.

After he left, I settled on the couch with my knitting. I tortured the yarn for about four rows before taking a cold shower. As I emerged from the bathroom, shivering, I realized that I could channel this energy for good. I was ready to kill someone.

CHAPTER ELEVEN

"Death. The eternal blink. The capricious dance of Now You Stop Moving Forever. Well, contrary to popular belief, death isn't just for dead people. It can happen to anyone."

—The Tick

All this sexual frustration needed to be flushed from my system, and I knew just how to do it. I would project it onto my job. At least, that's what I told myself as I crawled through the hedges behind Vic's house.

Dak had made good on his offer, so here I was, at 10 p.m.—on a school night, nonetheless—trying to find a way to off Leonard. There was no sign of life anywhere on the grounds. Even the evil Vivian wasn't home. But these hedges were scratching me something awful. Oh well, can't complain. Assassin Rule #2: If your hit is stupid enough to plant shrubbery, use it to your advantage. Of course the rule said nothing about how hot it was or how badly my arms were getting scraped.

I guess that particular rule is up to your own personal interpretation.

I found the back door without incident. Wouldn't you know the dumb-ass had a spare key under the doormat? His Witness Protection contact must have had a screw loose. I pulled the egg of Silly Putty (Assassin Fun Fact #2: You can use everyday things to your advantage) out of my purse and imprinted the key on both sides of it, then slid the putty back into my purse. After looking both ways (always look both ways—it works for more than crossing the street), I gingerly inserted the key into the doorknob and turned it.

A doorknob lock! Puhhhhleeeease. For a moment, I wondered if it wouldn't be more lucrative to hire on as this idiot's security.

I slipped into the house after replacing the key and locked the door behind me. My hands were sweating inside the latex gloves, but I knew better than to take them off. I remained crouched until my eyes adjusted to the dim interior. I was in the kitchen. And it was a mess. Now, I'm not the best housekeeper, but this was ridiculous. Dirty dishes were piled high in the sink, and the funk of sour food wafted from the disposal and garbage. Apparently, it was the maid's week off.

The bathroom was always the best

place to begin—especially if it was Vic's personal bathroom. I found it on the second floor. I adjusted my LED flashlight to red and searched his medicine cabinet. There was only one prescription bottle, for heart medication. So Leo had heart trouble, eh? That's good. I slipped one of the capsules out of the bottle and into my pocket, carefully replacing the lid.

From there, I quickly scanned each room in the house for entrances and exits, making a mental map. On the first floor, I found Leo's study. Bulls'-eye. And there, on the desk, was his appointment book, conveniently opened to tomorrow's activities. Hmmmm. Doctor's appointment in the morning. I was pretty sure Dr. Anwar was a cardiologist.

I checked out the kitchen before leaving. Vic had a proclivity for drinking. Woohoo! Drinking and heart medication don't mix. Looked like it would be an easy job after all.

Later, after sending my brother home and crawling into bed, I picked up a notebook and recorded everything I had seen. Once the job was done, the paper would be burned in the fireplace. No point in leaving any clues, eh?

I yawned and stretched. Not that I'd be considered a suspect. Nothing connected him to me. Of course, that would all depend on whether I could make it look like natural causes. I slid the notebook into the bottom drawer of my nightstand and locked it. I could work on it some more tomorrow.

"Hey, Mom," I said as I approached her in her backyard. According to the city's ordinance, homeowners could only have six-foot-high privacy fences. But Carolina Bombay's were eight feet tall. Funny story, that. Seems the city clerk used to date her in high school.

Mom turned around, brushing the honey blond hair from her eyes. In her hand was a Gil Hibben knife. Twenty feet behind her was a tall piece of plywood, sharp knives dotting its surface in a tight little group, dead center.

"Gin! I wasn't expecting you!" She gave me a warm hug, then collected her blades from the plywood. "How about some iced tea?"

We settled at the glass table on the patio just as Dad walked out with two tall glasses of iced tea. Blackberry Sage, no doubt. Mom was a creature of habit.

"You shouldn't drink loose tea," I started. "It would be easy for Uncle Lou to poison."

Mom arched her right eyebrow. "Not likely. The teaspoon and kettle are rigged to my and your father's biometrics. The wrong fingerprints and spikes plunge into your fingers."

That was Mom, always practical.

"Besides, I'm not a target," she added.

"And who is? Are you saying you know who's getting spanked at the family re-union?"

She shook her head. "You know I'm not privy to that information, Ginny. Only the Council knows."

I set my tea down. "Mom, why the meeting? What's going on?"

Carolina frowned, deep creases forming in the middle of her forehead. "I don't know. I really don't. And your grand-mother isn't very forthcoming either."

That would fit. Grandma believed in the system. She believed in the Council and its work. It would be impossible to get the info from her. And to be frank, she scared me shitless. Two years ago, I saw her throw a man forty years younger and three feet taller out a seventh-story win-dow. No, it wouldn't be in my best interest to ask.

"Any theories?"

"None. Sorry, honey. I wish I knew." Mom chewed her lip, and I could see she was worried. Every time there was a re-union, any one of us could be marked for termination. And I don't mean with a pink slip.

"So how's the job?" she asked, blithely changing the subject.

"Oh, easy. Shouldn't take any time." Vic had a doctor's appointment in two hours, and I wasn't going to miss it.

"Just see that you get it done before the trip. You don't want that hanging over your head."

She was right. The Council often used these occasions to interview members of the family to check up on their work. This was one performance evaluation everyone wanted to get right.

"I don't suppose it could be Richie who's in trouble?"

Mom laughed. "Wishful thinking, I'm afraid. Besides, Lou is his biggest fan. Nothing will happen to him."

Damn. You know how in every family there's one annoying cousin? One who has the most abrasive personality? Well, that was my cousin Richie. Arrogant, drooling, and I was quite sure, mentally retarded Richie. All my life the brat had tried to one-up me. He looked like Jabba the Hutt—but without the brains. Yet he thought he was God's gift to assassins.

I only had to see him once a year. Too bad it always ruined Christmas. He would follow me around, asking me questions with that nasal, high-pitched voice of his. Stuff like, "What are you driving?"

I'd tell him about my minivan and he'd

tell me the results of every gruesome accident there ever was in that particular vehicle. Then he'd call me an idiot and laugh.

Usually, I could ignore him. He was just so goddamned obnoxious. For some reason, he never did this to anyone in the family but me. Why? I'm not sure. I must be a target for people like him and Vivian to toy with.

Every five years, I hoped the Council would get sick of Richie, but they never did. As much of an asshole as he was, he never screwed up a job.

I caught my mom eyeing me. "No one knows the reason for the reunion, Ginny, so give it up."

"Fine." I slumped in my seat like a teenager. "It's just so weird."

Mom shook her head. "It's not that strange. I'm sure it's nothing."

But I knew she was lying. The last time the Council had called an early meeting, Lou took out my Aunt Virginia. Mom had to remember that.

"Are you ready for Romi's induction?" Mom asked.

"No. I have no idea what to do. How did you handle it when I was five?"

Mom smiled faintly. "Well, I just took you to the reunion and let the family explain it. You had no questions. Actually, you took the training rather well."

"You must have told me something."

She shook her head. "Not really. Once we got home, I started training you. You never once questioned it."

"And Dad was okay with it?" I asked.

"No. Did you expect him to be? But he got used to the idea."

I picked up my glass. "Don't they all."

"Aren't you glad you never told Eddie?"

The question stunned me. I'd never talked about it with her.

"Yes and no. I don't think it's easy to marry into the Bombay family and all of our perfectly normal 'traditions.'"

Mom laughed. "Enough of this. How did your date go with the Australian?"

I entered Dr. Anwar's office fifteen minutes before Vic was supposed to show up. I walked up to the receptionist and told her I was waiting for someone. She nodded without looking at me. The room was full of people, all busy ignoring me. I found the only two open seats and took one, placing my tote bag in the other. The mousey brown wig itched, but I didn't want to scratch it and risk moving it. I reached into my bag and pulled out a knitting project, waiting for good old Leonard to enter.

I loved knitting. When I say that, I didn't mean I enjoyed completing projects like sweaters and such. I just loved working with my hands on something less lethal. It was very calming. They say knitting is the new yoga.

A teenage boy with a Mohawk sat across from me, sneering. I'd seen that look before. Why was it a problem to knit in public?

"My grandma knits."

I ignored him.

"So what are you making, Grandma?" Mohawk's voice was ugly.

I arched my eyebrow. "A cashmere cock ring. Your grandma ever knit one of those?"

The kid's eyes grew wide, and he suddenly became very interested in a four-year-old issue of *Teen Vogue*.

As I said before, I loved knitting. I guess you could call me a knitting assassin. The tools were very useful. Once, I had to strangle a man with my circular needles. It hadn't even messed up the 15 rows of stitches I had on them. A solid pair of metal needles can be plunged into the eyes and brain. Remember Fun Fact #2? Everyday objects have so many uses.

The door opened and in walked Leonard. He checked in with the receptionist, then scanned the room. I gave him a brief smile and took my bag out of the chair next to me. It worked. He joined me.

"I hate waiting rooms," he grumbled to no one in particular. I didn't think I was in danger of liking him too much to kill him.

"Me too," I responded, my eyes still on my circular needles as the second row of stitches began to take shape.

"You can get sick from being here," he continued. "Too many people, too many germs."

I looked around, wondering how you could catch heart disease as an airborne virus. Now that would really be cool.

"Goddamned doctors," Vic mumbled. Oh, he was a winner.

"Mr. Burns?" A petite blond nurse stood in the open doorway with a clipboard. I watched as Leonard followed her into the back.

I was on my ninth row of stitches when he came back. I listened (without looking like I listened, of course) as the receptionist reminded him to fill his prescription. I waited a full twenty minutes before leaving the waiting room and heading to my car.

So what did I know? Vic had heart trouble and a lousy personality. This was enough information for me to finish the job. On my way home, I stopped at the health food store to pick up clear, empty gelatin capsules. The long-haired kid at the counter called me "dude" six times while ringing me up. That must've been a personal best for him. Usually I only got "dude" once. I didn't mind. As long as he didn't call me Virginia.

CHAPTER TWELVE

[Mr. Furious tries to balance a hammer on his head]
Mr. Furious: "Why am I doing this?"
The Sphinx: "If you can balance a tack hammer on your head, you will head off your foes with a balanced attack."
Mr. Furious: "And why am I wearing the watermelon on my feet?"
The Sphinx: [looks at the watermelon on Mr. Furious's feet] "I don't remember telling you to do that."
—Mystery Men

Setting up my plans for Vic's demise really helped to calm me down. There's kind of a green tea–Zen feeling to it all. *Calgon, take me away* and all that crap.

I needed to relax. After all, hell awaited me that afternoon. And it had nothing to do with my family . . . for once.

"Mrs. Bombay?" Emily O'Toole raised her hand. "Can I go to the bathroom?" Suddenly, all ten little girls raised their hands. Only five minutes into my first-ever Girl Scout meeting and I was already in over my head.

I looked through some papers they had given me down at the Scouts Council. "Um, yeah, just, er . . . take a buddy with you." They were gone before I looked up. Liv shrugged. Fat lot of help she was.

The screams from the girls' bathroom told me they weren't limiting their activities to the hygienic. Ten minutes later, I wrangled several soaking wet Daisy Scouts back into Romi's classroom.

"Okay," I began, "now that we know what *not* to do, I guess we can get started." I nodded to Liv and she proceeded to pass out the uniforms and handbooks.

"Here's your Daisy tunic and book. Remember to bring them to every meeting. Yes, Hannah?"

The tiny little girl put her hand down. "When are the meetings?"

"Oh, um . . ." I shuffled through the papers again in an attempt to look like I knew what I was doing. "Every other Tuesday, in here, right after school."

A discordant chorus of squeals pierced my eardrums. Apparently, they approved. Yippee.

Somehow, we managed to make daisies out of pipe cleaners before their moms came to get them. There I sat, covered in pipe cleaner fuzz and glue—which was really weird because we didn't even use glue. Liv took over at that point, handing out the application forms and giving instruction to the parents. I just sat there, like a lump, until it was over.

Liv flopped down into one of the teeny

tiny chairs next to the teeny tiny table. "Jesus. I'm glad that's over."

I looked at her. "Yeah. I didn't really expect that. How did it go?"

Liv rolled her eyes. "You led the meeting!"

"Oh, right," I responded. "Can we call that a meeting? I mean, it was more like a riot." I pictured Liv and myself in Riot Squad gear, approaching the kindergartners with plasticine shields and rubber bullets. For a moment, the idea appealed to me.

Liv frowned at the handbook. "It says here we have to teach them the Girl Scout Promise and they earn the petals for their daisy insignia through the meetings."

"You're just now reading the *Leader's Guide*?" I asked while pulling a clump of glue (and hair) off my head.

She looked alarmed. "It also says we're supposed to have training."

I perked up. "Maybe that's it. We should've done that first."

"Well, there's a training session for Daisy Leaders tomorrow night at the Lutheran church down the street from you. I'll call and sign us up."

I nodded, finally brave enough to rise from my itty, bitty chair. My muscles threatened to assassinate me. "Okay."

We gathered our things, straightened

the room and left. As I walked to my car I realized that for once I had no clue what in the hell I was doing. I could kill a man with my thighs, but I couldn't control a bunch of five-year-old girls. I think terrorist organizations would learn a lot from this kind of experience.

"Mommy?" Romi squeezed my hand, reminding me she was there. "That didn't go very well, did it?"

I slid open the passenger door and lifted her to her seat. "No. I guess not. But Liv and I are going to a workshop tomorrow night. We'll be okay."

The dubious look in my daughter's eyes made me realize she had little faith in me. Great. How could I train her to kill when I couldn't keep kindergartners from trashing the bathroom? And how do you get wet toilet paper off of the ceiling? Maybe they'd cover that tomorrow night.

The following evening at the Lutheran church, Liv and I sat up straight, eager to find out what we had done wrong. I was convinced that some hip, young Girl Scout Council professional would give us all the tools we needed to succeed.

Ergo, I wasn't prepared for the obese, elderly, wheezing woman who sat down across from us, reeking of beer and cigarettes. Wow, I guess scouting hadn't changed much since I was in it. All she needed to do now was tell me how great the handheld shower massage was for masturbation and I'd be right back in middle school.

"You two here for the workshop?" Eldamae Haskell eyed us with disdain.

"Um, is this for Daisy Scouts?" I spoke up. Hope refused to wane. Maybe we were in the wrong room?

"Yeah," she sputtered, coughing loudly. "Fill out these forms."

"A test?" I couldn't believe it. It was a test! How could we take a test on something we didn't know yet?

"It's to see what you know. You'll take the same test when we're through."

Liv asked, "And how long is the workshop?"

Eldamae gave a heavy, wet, rasping cough, "An hour . . . hour and a half at most."

"That's it?" I asked. "That's all the time it takes to teach us everything we need to know?"

"Yup," our teacher replied. She tossed us the papers and left, probably for a smoke break.

Actually, the test was pathetically easy. Upon Eldamae's return, we watched a videotape, possibly made in the early 1990s. The scene opened on some lovely, mythical mansion in a perfect world at the beginning of a scout meeting. A tight-lipped, professional, middle-aged woman with perfectly coiffed, glossy blond hair told the camera how she ran her meetings.

"First," she said with perfect diction, "you greet each girl at the door person-ally, discussing the subjects that interest her the most, and then guide her to a simple yet engaging activity to keep her busy until the other girls have arrived."

These Stepford children wore immacu-late clothes and quietly colored pictures promoting world peace and multicultural diversity. During the meeting, the kids quietly listened to everything the leader said, raising their hands if they wanted to speak.

Following that, they commenced learn-ing activities worthy of a postgraduate science seminar. Somehow, and without making a mess, they measured baromet-ric pressure using Saran Wrap, an empty two-liter pop bottle, and fingernail polish. Of course, the experiment opened their eager, young eyes to the possibilities and later in the meeting, they went on to cure cancer.

The problem of a disruptive child was addressed when a well-dressed Daisy in a clean tunic told another girl, "No, Darwin didn't favor Intelligent Design." This child

was deemed rude and the tight-lipped
leader whisked her aside to two chintz-
covered wingback chairs for a gentle chat.
The girl, realizing the error of her ways,
promised to move to India and take up
Mother Theresa's mantle in ridding society of poverty. She was then allowed to re-
join the group.

By the time parents in the video arrived
to pick up their angels, Liv and I were
completely slack jawed. The leader had
time to talk to each set of parents (that's
right, both mom and dad, dressed in
suits, came to pick up their darling)
about their daughter's progress. Once the
meeting ended, Tight-Lips told us that
the most important thing was to have
control of the meeting at all times. And
her hair was still perfect. Really. No pipe
cleaner fuzz or glue anywhere. Bitch.

Okay, so maybe I exaggerated a little
bit, but it was the most idiotic thing I'd
ever seen . . . and believe me, I'd seen stupid things in my line of work.

Eldamae rejoined us, handing us blank
copies of the same test we took prior to
the meeting. I had barely filled in my answers when she presented us with two
cards, signed by her.

"Keep these. Anytime you get training,
we'll add to it. Thanks for becoming a vol-
unteer." She packed up and was out the
door before I could say anything.

"That's all we need to know?" Liv asked in shock.

"Uh, I, er," I mumbled.

Neither one of us moved for maybe twenty minutes. We kept thinking someone would burst through the door, saying, "Just kidding!" This wonderful someone would hand over thick, colorful volumes that answered every question we had, and give us sage words of advice and an arsenal of Jedi mind tricks to use on our troop.

Instead, a thin, waspish woman poked her head in and told us to leave. The bridge club needed the room.

I wanted to kill her and Eldamae. And I probably could've gotten away with it too, if Liv hadn't dragged me out to the car.

"We are so screwed," I finally said after my fourth consecutive cup of coffee.

Liv nodded. "No shit. This is worse than the Falconi hit. Remember that?"

My turn to nod. How could I forget? Liv and I had just turned twenty-one and decided to take out this mob guy together. You know how it is when you're in your twenties—you think you're bulletproof?

Of course, we had done all the research. But while we were throttling him in his upstairs bedroom, a couple of Mafia-endorsed hit men were climbing the stairs to teach him the "forever lesson." We dove into a closet just before the door opened. Those bastards spent *two hours* in that room before leaving. Several times, they had approached the closet, but something stopped them. I was pretty sure my heart gave out three times that night. To this day, I still had an irrational hatred of closets.

"And those bastards took credit for the hit too! I've never seen Grandma that pissed off." I poured another cup of coffee in an attempt to drown that memory.

"Well, Gin, we'll just have to get through it." Liv slapped the table decisively.

"Great. At least we don't have another meeting for a while."

"Two weeks, right?" Liv asked.

"Yeah." Why was everything in two weeks?

"Shit, Gin! That's when we'll be in Santa Muerta!" Liv's eyes grew wide.

"We could always take them with us, like a camping trip."

She rolled her eyes. "Oh yeah, that would work."

"I'll send out a memo rescheduling the meeting. Besides, Santa Muerta looks better to me than that classroom."

Liv nodded, looked at her watch, said good-bye and fled.

As I locked up, I realized postponing the meeting was a pretty easy decision. Hmmm . . . watching a family member die or spending an hour with the Daisies, who by the way had *not* seen the video.

I drifted off to sleep, fantasizing about the many uses of duct tape and psychotropic drugs.

CHAPTER THIRTEEN

"Mr. Pugh. Here is your arsenic, dear.
And your weedkiller biscuit . . ."
—Dylan Thomas, *Under Milkwood*

I was running out of time. I had to get rid
of Vic before the reunion. My to-do list
had grown to epic proportions:
1. The Job
2. The Reunion
3. Begin Romi's Training
4. Begin Poppy's Training (or put carpet cleaner on speed dial)
5. Learn to Run Daisy Meetings (without stun guns)
6. Order four Dozen Scary Halloween Cookies

As you can see, I had my priorities. If I
could get the job done before the trip, I
was pretty sure I could handle whatever
got tossed at me, with the possible excep-
tion of #5. Oh, and the stun guns would
be for the girls.

I had everything I needed. I had managed to whip up a lethal lookalike heart medication and fill the empty gel caplets I bought at the health food store. With just one dose, Vic would find his blood pressure boiling and his heart beating in time to a calypso death spiral. To a bored coroner on a Friday night before quittin' time, it would look as though there had been a simple (albeit deadly) screwup at the pharmacy. Now all I had to do was break back into the house and "refill" Vic's prescription bottle.

A couple of days ago, I'd taken the Silly Putty out of its shell, carefully slicing it in half so I had the two sides of the key impression facing up. Once it hardened, I poured in a special resin I invented (all this and good looks too—can you believe it?) and allowed it to set. After joining the two resin key sides together, I used the key grinder to fine-tune it for one-time use. That's all the resin would hold up for, but it was all I really needed.

- ☠ Bulk order of Silly Putty . . . $20.00
- ☠ Key grinder purchased from eBay . . . $55.00
- ☠ Seeing Vic's obituary in the paper and easing any family conflict in the process . . . Priceless.

Dad agreed to come over and watch Romi and Poppy since it was a school night. I waited until my daughter was asleep, then took a shower with un-

scented soap, put on unscented deodor-
ant (the invisible kind, of course), then
slipped out of the house dressed in black
yoga pants, a black long-sleeved T-shirt,
black socks and shoes, carrying a bag
with, you guessed it, a black stocking cap
and latex gloves.

I really hated latex gloves. It was like
when you pump gas and get some on your
hands and you smell those chemical
fumes all day. I *hated* that.

Where was I? Oh yeah, in the hedges
behind Vic's house. And no, I didn't just
go over there cold. According to Liv's research, Vic was going to the annual meeting for his company. It was my only
opportunity. The bastard didn't give to
charity or make appearances at public
events. Creep.

The key turned noiselessly in the lock,
and I shut the door behind me. Ugh, the
kitchen again. Apparently, Vic had at-
tempted some minor cleaning. This guy
was a slob. Good for me in that he would
be careless with his medication and probably ignore the symptoms of his heart attack. Bad for me because it smelled like
he had some prehistoric eggs rotting in
the sink.

I moved quickly up the stairs to his
bathroom. It only took a few seconds to
dump his meds into my bag and refill it
with my own, personal pain*killer*.

I was just about to head down the stairs (and perform a little celebratory dance in my head), when I heard the clink of glass breaking in the kitchen. I froze in midstep. Did Vic have a cat? There'd been no evidence of that. And the way this guy kept house, I would have smelled a neglected litter box.

For a moment, I wondered if he had mice. With the condition of the kitchen, I wouldn't be surprised if he had dog-size cockroaches. I backed away from the staircase slowly, leaning against the wall and waited impatiently. That's right, I was an impatient assassin. Several minutes passed without incident. *Okay, mice it is*, I thought as I gently slipped down the stairs, careful not to tread on the usually squeaky middle part of each step.

My eyes were adjusting to the darkness somewhat, and I was just about to pass the study when I saw it: the silhouette of a man standing at Vic's desk. Shit. I slipped to the other side of the doorway unnoticed, I thought. After a few scary seconds of crawling through the disgusting kitchen, I slipped out the open door. And into the shrubs.

The brick wall snagged my clothes. Who the hell was that? Was it Vic? No, a man turns on the lights when he enters his own home and definitely shuts and locks the door behind him. A burglar?

Maybe. It was a pretty ostentatious house. I could call 911. But that would be stupid, on the remote chance they might check his meds. *Okay, Gin, just go home.*

Was I being followed? The idea froze inside me as a lump in my throat. Something was up with the family. Was I under suspicion? I slid further down the wall, remaining in the shrubbery. If anyone was checking up on me, they might have left someone outside to watch for my retreat. I kind of hoped it was Evil Cousin Richie so I could kill him once and for all.

I waited for the shadow to exit the house and followed him as he walked around to the front yard. From my vantage point in the hedge, I watched until he disappeared down the street.

"And you say he was dressed like you?" Dad asked me once I got back to the house. We were sharing a bottle of wine in the kitchen, and I told him what had happened. I was boiling down Vic's meds in a pot on the stove. Once dissolved, I'd flush the water and stick the pot in the dishwasher on "high."

I nodded. "Yup. All in black."

Dad leaned back in his chair, thoughtfully. I, however, had just started to notice a particular odor souring the room.

"Burnt popcorn? Dad!" Was there any

smell more obnoxious than burnt popcorn? Even worse, it was done on purpose. Dad's favorite snack was seriously
charred popcorn. Mom couldn't get him
to give it up. I had a popcorn ban on my
house because of it, but apparently he
had ignored that and smuggled some in.

"What?" He feigned innocence. "Romi
wanted some."

"Dad! You promised!" I whined.

He smiled. "Okay, never again."

"You know what will happen to you if
you go back on that promise!" I threatened
as I rummaged under the sink for a can of
Ozium. Of course, my threats bore all the
weight of a feather. Mom had threatened
him for years with all kinds of nasty shit
and he never listened.

I sprayed the air liberally. Just a word
of advice, never spray it in an enclosed
car while you're sitting there. It dis-
places oxygen, I think. *Bad* trip, that
was. Great, now all of a sudden I sounded
like Yoda.

"So, you don't think it's family. . . ."
Dad resumed our previous discussion.

"I have no idea." I squinted at him. "You
don't know something, do you?"

He laughed. "No, I stay out of the family
stuff. Life's a little saner if you forget who
the Bombays are."

I chewed my lip. "I guess it must be

weird for an outsider, huh?" I wondered about people who married in. They received their Bombay Wake-Up Call when they were adults. But we had it spoon-fed like it was a normal thing at the tender age of five.

"It was, at first. Now I just ignore it and spend the money. Scruples are for suckers anyway," he said with a wink. "I'm really proud of you, honey."

I responded to this Kodak moment by rolling my eyes. "Oh, great. My dad's proud of me 'cause I can kill people real good."

"That's not what I mean," he continued, "I mean it's hard to take on the family legacy and find a way to live with it."

"So . . . you're not proud of the fact I can fling an ice pick fifty yards into a man's eye socket?" After all, *I* was proud of that.

"Well, I guess there's that too." Dad rubbed his chin. "But you've made a good life out of what was given to you. You're raising a daughter alone. And you managed to get through sixteen years of education without killing any of your bullies."

"Sure, when you put it that way." I refilled his wineglass, then my own. "I'd like to think Eddie would've taken the news as well as you did."

Dad looked at me, "Don't get me wrong,

Ginny, I really liked Ed. But there was a part of me that was a little relieved that he died before you told him. I don't know how he would've handled it."

For some reason, that made sense. In a sick, thank-God-your-husband-got-cancer-before-you-had-to-tell-him-you're-a-killer sort of way. But speculation about Eddie wasn't the problem in front of me.

"Look," Dad said, "why don't you get in the car and drive around Vic's neighborhood? See if there are cops or something else. I can see you aren't going to sleep until you know what's going on."

So that's what I did. First I changed my clothes; then I went to the convenience store to pick up a half-gallon of milk (as my alibi for what I was doing out so late). I cruised slowly past Vic's house and circled it once. Nothing. With a sigh of relief I drove two blocks back to my house, dismissed my father and chucked the milk into the fridge. I began the ritual cleaning of my break-in gear, scraping all dirt from my shoes into the disposal and rinsing the soles, throwing the clothes into the washer and wrapping the gloves inside of what appeared to be a used maxi pad (doctored with red food coloring, of course). You know, the usual stuff.

It was past midnight when I finished my shower, checked my arms and legs for tell-tale scrapes from the shrubs, and crawled into bed. Hopefully, Vic's death would take place within twenty-four hours and all would be well. Just another random day in the life of Gin Bombay, All-American Assassin-Next-Door.

CHAPTER FOURTEEN

"Forgiveness is between them and God. It's my job to arrange the meeting."

—Creasy, *Man on Fire*

I usually give my "concoctions" a few days to work. Sometimes, Vic is the type who doesn't take his medication regularly. So I decided to put my worries on the shelf and focus on prepping the house for Romi and Alta's training. Liv and I worked to set up the basement in my house for *Little Girls Gone Lethal*.

For an entire day (Dak picked up the girls after school and kept them occupied), we unpacked the new stuff and organized it. I installed locked wooden cabinets to hold the garrotes, dummies and knives. Liv bought a kids' chemistry set so it would look amateurish (unlike the primo stuff in my workshop). When we were done, we sat back and admired our work.

Liv handed me a bottle of beer and sat on the new sofa I had put downstairs.

"Wow," I noted, "looks like a deranged playroom."

Liv nodded. "It does, doesn't it? Maybe we shouldn't have gone so crazy with the Disney Princess theme?"

"Well, it does give it a certain childlike atmosphere. It just looks like this is the part of Cinderella's castle she didn't visit so much."

"The torture room?" Liv asked.

"At least there's no Iron Maiden." I took a swallow of beer.

"True." Liv rubbed her chin. "But I think it's safe to say that we should have the Daisy Troop Christmas Party at my house."

"Deal. By the way, where's Dak?" I looked at my watch. "It's getting late."

As if on cue, peals of giggling laughter erupted above us. Liv and I moved up the stairs quickly. I was just plugging in the combination code to lock the door when the girls came running in.

"I don't think they'll want dinner. . . ." Dak smiled.

"We had *lots* of ice cream!" Romi yelped.

"I can see that," I said as I took the dish towel to her face.

"Uncle Dak *rocks!*" Alta shouted, and the two danced circles around their hero.

"Great. Thanks, little brother." I wasn't smiling.

"No problem. Let me know if you guys want me to unfairly overdose your kids with sugar again." Dak grinned, then fled before I could kill him.

Liv and I did the only thing we could do: We took our beer bottles and two squealing kids into the backyard to burn off some steam.

"When should we tell them?" Liv asked quietly.

"I don't know. I'm afraid to do it before the reunion. Romi already tells her teacher too much stuff. The other day, she told her that I gave birth to a puppy."

Poppy opened one bulging eye, then went back to snoring on Liv's lap.

"Okaaay. So, when?" Liv stroked the pup between the ears.

"What did our parents do with us?"

"You know," Liv said.

"Uh, no, I can't remember. Seriously. How did they break us in?"

She looked at me for a minute, probably wondering if I was teasing her. "They just had us attend the ritual. Then my dad and your mom took us to the bungalows overnight to explain things to us. You really don't remember?"

Actually, I didn't. And I'd be lying if I said I wasn't a little more than alarmed by that.

I took a swig of beer. The girls were
swinging so high I thought they might go
over the top any minute now. Thanks, Dak.

"Let's do the same thing, then. That
way, we can keep all discussion about it
on the island until we return."

Liv smiled. "I'll reserve one of the bungalows. We can make pizza. Like a little
sleepover!"

"Yeah," I said slowly, eyes still on the
girls. "The sleepover where instead of using the Ouija board or giving ourselves
pedicures, we get to tell the girls how to
kill a man using just your index finger."

"Well, that's a little more advanced. We
might want to save that nugget until at
least second grade," Liv responded.

"Good point." I drained my beer. "We
probably shouldn't get ahead of ourselves."

We sat outside until dusk, making plans
for the training when we returned from
Santa Muerta. Eventually, I wrestled my
little sugar junkie into the tub, then into
bed.

I was just picking up my knitting when
the doorbell rang. With a frown, I hoisted
the comatose Poppy from my lap and
checked the security cameras.

"Diego!" I cried out, pleasantly surprised to see the hunky Australian on my
doorstep. Swooning when I saw the bouquet of yellow roses in his right hand. Of
course, I would have been just as happy

with a bouquet of condoms. Maybe even happier.

"Sorry to show up unannounced like this." He kissed my lips gently as I ushered him into the house. "But I just wanted to see you, and I couldn't wait until tomorrow night."

I put the flowers in water and returned to the couch. Diego scooped up Poppy and placed her on his lap. The little whore went crazy.

"You knit?" He pointed at my needles.

"Yeah. Just rectangles really."

Diego raised his eyebrows. "Rectangles?"

"Well, I don't have the ambition to try socks or sweaters. I really just enjoy the mechanics of it. So I stick to the easy stuff . . . scarves and afghans." I suppose that made me sound like an idiot. But if he were smart, Diego wouldn't make fun of a woman holding potentially lethal needles.

"Is Romi asleep?" he ventured.

I nodded. "Flat out like a lizard drinking."

Diego laughed. "Where did you hear that? I thought only Aussies said that."

I couldn't tell him I once had to "take care" of an Australian gun runner, so I lied. "I had a friend in college from Perth."

Diego gently pushed Poppy aside, then pulled me onto his lap and kissed me.

Somehow I knew that this was going further than before. Diego didn't seem to be that confident; in fact, he seemed like he'd be perfectly happy just kissing.

But I wanted more. I wanted to make love to him. We'd kept the relationship shallow so far, but now I interpreted his restraint as Diego treading lightly on my feelings. He never pressured me, and was careful, as if he thought this was my first time since Ed died.

I felt the pressure of his lips against mine, and my stomach ached. It *was* my first time since Ed. For a moment, I almost pulled away. My heart fluttered, and my head panicked (thanks a lot, guys) and I questioned myself. What in the hell was I doing?

Sure, we had a lot in common and there was all that volcanic chemistry. Was I ready for this? Sex had always been with someone I cared about. But I cared about Diego.

As if he knew what I was thinking, Diego began to gently stroke my back. Damn, he was good. No, he was great. He was perfect. And I wanted him.

So that's it then, eh? I just decide to go for it? Yes! No more celibacy for me! Although it gave me the tension I needed for my job, it sucked. I didn't just want to make out with Diego, I wanted to make love to him.

I needed to feel alive, not just pretend I was. I craved the things that used to make me feel like a woman: the heart palpations, tingling flesh, stomach spinning and rubbery knees that all led to the hard knot of arousal. What if I got hit by a delivery truck tomorrow? I knew that sounded cliché, but hell, my family couldn't take longevity for granted.

A flood of warmth filled my body like hot water. I guess that was the physical side of me saying, *Duh!* I needed more from Diego than just hot sex. And he was waiting for me to let him know that.

I started to unbutton his shirt. Diego pulled back, a questioning look in his eyes.

"Are you okay with this? We don't have to . . ." His voice trailed off.

"I know. I want to," I murmured. Inside I felt all squishy. How could I let this guy walk out of here without a "happy ending"?

Diego smiled and pulled me toward him, his lips trailing down my neck. Our clothes pretty much disintegrated at that point, and a flood of raw emotion seemed to make all of my senses tingle.

Diego pulled back. "I know it's been a long time for you. We can take it slowly . . ."

"No." I shook my head. "I don't want to waste time."

He laughed, and I started to get nervous. His body was lean, hard (in all the right places). Mine was not. Childbirth had given me stretch marks that everyone lied about in saying they would fade in time. I didn't have washboard abs or flawless skin. Hell, I couldn't even remember when I'd last shaved my legs!

"You are so beautiful, Gin." Diego's eyes seemed to glow as he appraised my body.

I made a vain attempt to suck in my stomach, and he smiled, pulling my arms open. "I mean it. You're lovely."

With that simple statement, all my worries flew away. He didn't care what I looked like! Maybe he was into soccer moms. It didn't matter. He could have spoken Klingon and I would've loved it.

It goes without saying that he was *amazing!* I didn't know if Australians had some special sexual know-how, or if bodyguards learned a few extra moves in their training, but *damn!* I refused to believe it was because it had been so long for me.

Remember how it felt when you were a teenager in the back of your dad's car? The excitement of discovering your body and exploring his? It was like that. Except without the fumbling as he tried to undo my bra. Diego definitely had no trouble with that. In fact, every move he made was sure, desperate, as if his sur-

vival depended upon it. I could relate a little to that.

I was pretty sure my body exploded. I
knew my heart did. I didn't realize how
much I had been missing. As an added
bonus, the orgasm produced this feeling
of euphoria I hadn't felt in a long time.
Well, at least not since I'd had that Godiva
Belgian Chocolate ice cream a few months
ago. There was a fleeting thought of Ed,
and I realized that while I had lost part of
what had been "us," I'd found part of me.
Somehow, I knew he would've approved.

As we lay naked and panting on the
couch, Diego ran his forefinger down the
middle of my nose. His smile told me the
sex meant something to him too. His
smile was softer, warmer. It delivered a
gut-twisting impact.

"Thank you," I said.

"I think I should be the one thanking
you," he responded. "But I do have a
question."

I arched my right eyebrow. *Please don't
ask me anything personal and ruin the
moment!* I wasn't ready for an in-depth
conversation on our feelings.

"Do you even have a bedroom?"

I looked at him curiously. "Yes, of
course I do. Why?"

Diego grinned. "Well, it's just that
we've fooled around twice, both times in

your living room. I just wondered if you had a bed."

I frowned. "You don't like my couch?"

He laughed. "I wouldn't care if we had sex on a tractor. I just wondered if there was a reason why we didn't utilize a more comfortable place. Somewhere I wouldn't get rug burns on my knees."

"I don't know. I guess that's a good point. I just hadn't thought about it."

"Maybe it has something to do with your late husband? I can completely understand if that's it."

Hmmm . . . it would be easy to tell him that I wasn't ready to share my late husband's bed with him. But was that really the case? Or was I just into living room sex?

"Honestly, Diego, it never occurred to me. That's all."

He looked at me for a moment before responding, "Okay. I'll buy that." Diego shook his finger at me mockingly. "But next time, let's use it." He rubbed his back. "I'm not as young as I used to be. These Kama Sutra positions don't work on a loveseat."

"Why do you think they call it a loveseat?" I punched him in the arm playfully.

Diego responded by pulling me in for a kiss. "Who cares? Next time, let's use your bed."

"It's a deal," I said, snuggling against him. I made a mental note to wash the sheets and clean the bedroom. I was just happy there would be a next time.

CHAPTER FIFTEEN

"I need a break. There's no retirement home for assassins, is there? Archery at four. Riflery at five?"
—Julian Noble, *The Matador*

Leonard Burns's obituary was small, with an accompanying photo (I guess the witness protection program gives up when their clients die), but it gave me a warm, fuzzy feeling to think that monkey was off my back. Of course, I didn't attend the funeral. That would be stupid. Police statistics show that a murderer almost always attends the funeral of his or her victim.

I'd been searching the news for the past two days for any sign of an investigation. Usually, though, the Feds don't like bad publicity.

On the other hand, the big red "X" on my calendar marking the trip to the family island was getting closer. Actually, there wasn't much time before we'd have to leave. I'd spent the last few days packing for Romi and me, securing our airline tickets to L.A., where we'd board the family's private jet to the island.

Romi's teacher was okay with pulling her out of school. Teachers always seem to melt when the words "Disney World" are mentioned. What was I supposed to do? Tell her the truth? *Actually, Liv and I are taking our daughters to begin their training as assassins. If I were you, I'd make my seating arrangements carefully in the future.* Liv and I had arranged to travel together—more to provide a united front than anything else.

The hardest part was finding a swimsuit that took off twenty pounds, reduced wrinkles in my face and made the color of my eyes pop. The only people who'd see me in it were Liv and the girls when we had our sleepover at the bungalows, but I didn't want to take any chances.

Diego had to go out of town on business with his client for a few days and my body was going through sex withdrawal. Oh well. I'd waited this long, I could wait some more. He would get back two days before I left for Santa Muerta. At least that was something.

All in all, I guess things were going very well. I checked a couple things off my list: the job and ordering the Halloween cookies way in advance (thereby annoying the bakery), and things were going well with Diego. So I celebrated with lunch at my favorite outdoor bistro. I soaked up the early autumn sunshine, a juicy half-pound cheeseburger with cross-cut fries and a bottle of beer, while engrossed in a new book.

This is probably why I didn't notice that I was no longer alone, at first.

"Jesus, Dak! You know better than to sneak up on me!" I was a little concerned that he always seemed to know where I was.

The bastard helped himself to my fries, his hand moving out of my reach before I could put a fork through it.

"Well, I have been doing it all my life, you know. I have a lot of experience."

The waitress appeared immediately. Something about Dak's pheromones usually brought every woman within a one-mile radius. It was like a dog whistle or something. I waited as he ordered the same thing I had. In spite of my mother's excellent cooking and firm belief in the food pyramid, my brother and I had a connoisseur-like devotion to greasy meat.

"So what's up?" I slid my book into my purse.

Dak feigned incredulity. "Can't a man just want to have lunch with his big sister? Honestly, Gin, you're too paranoid."

I laughed, "Okay. But you have to split a dessert with me."

Dak took another handful of my fries. "It's a deal."

Actually, it was nice. My brother and I had always enjoyed each other's company. Not that we hadn't fought as kids—even normal siblings do that. We're just very close. There's something about dealing in death that brings out the maternal in me.

I put the last forkful of chocolate cheesecake in my mouth and savored it. Damn, that was good. Dak had graciously allowed me the last bite. Maybe he wasn't such a bastard after all.

"Oh," Dak said, wiping his mouth, "I almost forgot this." He pulled a manila envelope out of his jacket and handed it to me.

I didn't have to examine it to know what it was. "You're kidding," I managed weakly. He was kidding, right?

Dak shook his head, no smile on his face this time. "Sorry. The Council wants you to handle it."

"I never get two jobs in the same month! No one does!"

Dak studied me. "Well, this time you do. And they want it done before the reunion."

"What?" I shrieked. "Wait a minute! This is a joke, right? You're just messing with me. That's it!"

"Nope. Believe me, Gin, I'd do it for you if I could. But Mom said I can't."

That's it. She is sooooo not getting a Mother's Day card this year.

"Just get it over with and you won't have to worry about it at the reunion. In fact," Dak rubbed his chin, "you probably don't have to worry about anything at all with the family. No one's ever been handed two jobs like this before."

The faraway look in his eyes made me wonder what he was thinking, but then I snapped back to reality. As I drove home, I couldn't help thinking he was right. Obviously, the Council trusted me to take care of two jobs in a very short period of time. I suppose in some twisted way, this was my chance at an excellent job performance review.

Once back at home, I tore open the envelope, glancing nervously at the surveillance cameras. I only had four days to complete this mission. Dak had agreed to watch Romi for me so I could do surveillance tonight.

"That's weird," I thought aloud. This Vic lived in the same neighborhood as the last one. That almost . . . no, that never happened. In fact, I didn't think I'd ever had two jobs in the same county before.

According to the dossier, Vic Jr. lived across the street from the other Vic. He was an executive of the same company, for Christ's sake! Bob Turner ranked very high on the corporate ladder on an international level. And he'd been very naughty—using company profits to support terrorists in South America. I didn't know if the contract came from the corporation, the government or a combination of both. And I didn't care. I just wanted to knock him off and get it over with. In fact, I kind of missed the days when the only thing I avoided was Vivian.

Oh well, let's get on with it, Gin. I shoved a baseball cap on my head, shoved my keys into my pocket and drove off to check out Vic Jr.'s house.

I only had one opportunity to drive past it. This neighborhood had seen a lot of me in the last week, so the jogging pretext was out. Visiting Vivian twice in one month, considering I'd avoided her all of my life, would raise suspicion. In fact, my car had been on this street one too many times already.

The house was small. A one-story, brick Tudor. This guy outranked the first job, but he had a tiny house. Go figure. People are weird. I was surprised to see that the house was the same one I stopped in front of to take a picture of Burns' house.

While Vic Jr.'s proximity might be seen as an advantage, and I was getting to know the neighborhood really well, it screwed me too. Everything I did would have to be under the cover of darkness. I couldn't have any questions as to why, after ten years, I started hanging out on this particular block. In fact, I was pretty sure it was risky just driving by once.

Back at home, as I turned on the computer, I sketched the house on paper. One-story houses were awesome to break into. And you didn't have to worry about escaping out of the second- or third-story windows. On the other hand, small houses sucked because there were few places to hide if my target came home suddenly.

There wasn't much about Vic Jr. on the Internet. He'd been posted in virtually every international office his company had. I couldn't find anything about extracurricular activities. No presence on any boards of directors, no civic clubs, no wife and no kids. This guy was just a loner who preferred not to draw any attention to himself.

Okay. He kept a low profile. That was perfect for his racket. But it also meant he was probably very careful with his security. And while I was grateful not to have to worry about a wife, kids or pets, there was the even greater risk that this guy played things close to the vest. Chances were, he had an excellent security system and knew how to use it.

In other words, this gig would *not* be easy. And while I appreciated the Council's confidence in me, there was no room for error and little time for planning. Fantastic.

Dak arrived as promised, looking sheepish. I knew he felt bad about being the messenger—well, of death, actually. I gave him instructions, donned my assassin gear and slipped out to go to work.

Vic Jr.'s house was quiet. As I approached from the side, I threw a pinecone next to the house. Motion sensitive lights snapped on immediately, flooding the area with bright white light. Shit. And this guy didn't have shrubs anywhere either. I waited to see if someone would investigate, but no one did.

After a few minutes, lights came on inside the house. I recognized they were on a timer. I'd seen too many of these things in my line of work. So no one was home, but they wanted me to think they were. Okay.

I sidled up to the back door, lock picks in hand. Not to brag, but I was really good at picking locks. And I knitted these cute little cozies for each tool to keep them from jangling together and making noise. It took a few, well-lit moments to unlock the deadbolt, and I slipped into the house. Obviously, this guy was serious about security. That deadbolt was a real bitch.

I only had a few seconds to locate and dismantle any alarm system. Most systems allowed a ten-second leeway for the owner to get in the door and to the system before it went off. I was pretty sure this guy had one. Fortunately, I had something better.

A couple of years back, one of my cousins invented an ultrasonic frequency blocker. It took a long time, but she managed to come up with a device that could eliminate alarm noise by masking it in the air. It's kind of the same technology that air fresheners use when they destroy the odor instead of masking it. Plus, it took out any signal to 911 or the security company. We Bombays were nothing if not thorough.

Okay, I was inside and had taken out the alarm. I began my search of the house. Damn. This bastard was clean. Unlike his unfortunate neighbor across the street, Vic Jr. kept his house spotless. In fact, it didn't look like anyone really lived here at all. No garbage, no dirty dishes, no dust, no personal knick-knacks. The fridge was full of hermetically sealed health food.

The bathroom was even worse. This son-of-a-bitch was so healthy he wasn't on any medication. I couldn't even find a bottle of aspirin. Panic started to rise, but I fought it. After thirty minutes in the house, I couldn't find one single way to poison this guy. He even drank bottled water! There was no unopened food I could tamper with, the surfaces were too clean to leave toxic residue anywhere, and he had no health problems.

Shit. I locked up the house and headed home. It looked like I'd be doing this one the old-fashioned way—barging in and plugging him in person. At least when they investigated, the police might discover his links to terrorism. That would send them on all kinds of wild goose chases, leaving me virtually clear.

"Nothing? There was nothing?" Dak raised his eyebrows. "Are you sure?"

I nodded. "Absolutely. I couldn't find a goddamned thing I could use to make it look natural."

Dak fidgeted with his coffee cup. "What are you going to do?"

"Do it a la Arnold Schwarzenegger, I guess. I'll probably have to use a ski mask and leave behind something to incriminate the Shining Path terrorists or something."

Dak looked at me. "I know you don't like doing things that way. Can I help?"

"I'd love to say yes, but I don't think so. Obviously, the family wanted me to do it myself."

My brother gave me a hug and we said our good-byes. I sat down on the couch and picked up my knitting. It helped me think sometimes. Poppy rolled lazily onto her back, but upon receiving no belly scratch, she rolled back over and went to sleep. She didn't have to kill anything but time.

CHAPTER SIXTEEN

"There's always free cheese in a mousetrap."
—Longbaugh, *The Way of the Gun*

I spent the next morning researching South American terrorists on the Internet. I had a few ideas of how to implicate them at the scene of the crime, but nothing else. I called Vic Jr.'s company from a pay phone, asking for Turner, and was told he was out of the office until tomorrow. Great. That meant I had only one day to hit him and hop the plane to L.A. with Romi.

By the afternoon, I had nothing. Not even a shred of confidence that I could do this. I'd only gunned down my prey once. And that was very, very messy. It all worked out in the end, but it was so much easier when you didn't have to witness the Vic's demise in person. That and it's impossible to get brain matter out of cashmere. I'd had to burn a perfectly good sweater.

The next morning, I dropped Romi off at school. *Bye, honey. Mommy's off to kill a man, and tomorrow after school we'll hop on a plane for the reunion. Okay?*

I had just gotten home when the door-bell rang. I checked my surveillance monitors, and my heart nearly stopped beating.

"Um, hello?" I said to Vic Jr., as he stood on my porch. This was too weird. Funny, I didn't remember using a hallu-cinogenic inhalant this morning.

"May I come in, Ms. Bombay?" Vic Jr. asked.

I nodded and ushered him in, looking to see if anyone saw us. Normally, I didn't let strange men in the house, but this was too good to be true. As I closed the door, my heart bounced back to life. This was it! My hit had come to my house! I could rub him out here!

"Can I help you, Mr. . . . ?" I fished for his name to confirm it was really him.

"Turner. And yes, you can. May we sit down?"

Where were my manners? Well, I could offer him coffee, but that would leave DNA evidence that he had been in my house.

I nodded and led him to the family room. Vic Jr. sat on the couch.

"How did you know my name, and what can I do for you?" I asked.

Turner laughed. It was a hard, cold

laugh. Killing this bastard was going to be no problem.

"Let's just say we both have colleagues within the government."

My mind scrambled to process this. Was he threatening me? Did he know about the Bombays? How?

"I'm sorry, Mr. Turner, but you show up at my house unannounced, and presume to have some connection to me?"

He leaned closer. "I know who you are and what you are."

I stiffened. "I don't think so. You're going to have to explain to me what you're doing here."

He leaned back, crossing his arms. "You and I have a common connection. I wanted to let you know."

Okay, obviously he knew something, but he wasn't going to tell me.

"I don't know what you're talking about," I said, standing. "But it feels like you're threatening me."

Turner remained seated. "No, not at all. I just think someone like you could be useful to me in the future."

Did he really know something? Was he blackmailing me? Because I hated that!

"How about I get us some coffee and we can discuss it, then?" I waited for his approval, and once he nodded, I walked around the couch, behind him. After all, he didn't know where the kitchen was.

He was just sitting there, probably considering evil corporate thoughts, when I looped my set of circular knitting needles around his neck, twisted the ends together and pulled.

Vic Jr. struggled immediately, but I'd done this too many times not to succeed. I could feel him panic as he clawed at the cord around his neck. He pulled out several rows of stitches in a vain attempt to remove the garrote. I put my knee into the back of the couch and used my weight to pull harder while pushing him down to hold him in place. He was at a complete disadvantage. It took only about twenty seconds before he was unconscious, but I kept up the pressure for two or three more minutes until I was sure he was dead.

I pushed his body onto the floor and checked for a pulse. There was no heartbeat. And I sure as hell wasn't going to use CPR to revive him. Vic Jr. had walked into my house, trying to surprise and trap me. Stupid man, underestimating his opponent like that.

I looked at my knitting. The yarn was stretched out in several places. Damn. I'd really liked that scarf. Oh well, I'd have to destroy it now. Chances were there were skin cells in the fibers that would match his DNA.

I'd never done a job in my own house before. The job was over and I was free, but I was pissed that he had the opportunity to choose the time and place.

Damn, now I had to dispose of the body too. That would be a problem. Well, the Council said I couldn't have help killing the guy, but it said nothing about help getting rid of his remains. I was just about to dial the phone when the doorbell rang.

What the hell? This would be an inopportune moment for the Avon lady to visit. I looked into the monitors and this time, my heart stopped beating for real.

"Diego!" I tried to say happily. I still couldn't believe I'd answered the door.

He kissed me. "Unfortunately, this isn't a social call. My client ditched me while I was in the shower, left a note about going for a walk. I'm looking for him and thought I'd kill two birds with one stone by checking on you."

"Um, your client?" I said uneasily.

"Yeah. His name's Turner." He pulled out a picture. "Have you seen him around?"

Sure, he's dead in my living room. I just got done strangling him. Why?

I stared at the photo. "No, haven't seen anyone like him."

"I'll find him. It's just weird. He's never done that before."

So this was what real panic felt like. I'd

just killed my boyfriend's client. Diego was supposed to protect Vic Jr. from assassins like me. I was pretty sure if he found out, our relationship would be over.

"Yeah, well, you know clients. Sometimes they just want a little alone time," I managed.

Diego kissed me once more, then set out to see if the dead man in my house was wandering the neighborhood. I locked the door and called Dak and Liv.

I watched as my baby brother walked slowly around the dead guy. Liv stood with her hands on her hips, brows furrowed as if she were trying to decide which wallpaper should go in here. I failed to mention that Turner was Diego's client.

"What about the river?" Liv suggested.

Dak shook his head. "No, I think we use that too much already. We could take him out to a cornfield somewhere."

Liv snorted. "Sure, if you want to leave tire tracks in the mud."

I, at least, was grateful to have an attached garage so we could put him in my trunk, sight unseen.

"How about the limestone quarry?" Liv offered.

"We'll have to wait until late tonight," Dak said.

I shook my head vigorously. "No way. He's getting out of here right now!"

My brother and cousin looked startled at my reaction. But none of us had ever taken out a Vic in our own home before.

"Okay," Dak started slowly, "let's put him in the trunk of your sedan. I'll take him now, and dump him later tonight."

"Fine!" I was actually shaking. Everything seemed to go to hell. I had killed Diego's client in my house! That couldn't be good.

Liv and I rolled Turner's body into a plain white blanket. We wore gloves to avoid leaving anything on him. Dak and I carried him to the trunk, laying him out on a plain blue tarp. I didn't want any evidence in the car.

After Dak left, Liv and I vacuumed the living room—carpet, furniture and all—emptied the vacuum canister into an empty garbage bag, and cleaned the canister with bleach. I just needed to get the garbage out and everything would be fine.

I poured myself a glass of wine while Liv settled for a beer.

"Gin, why was Vic in your house?" Liv asked.

"I don't know. He just showed up. Maybe I have good karma or something."

"Right." She frowned. "So why was he here?"

I drained my wineglass and poured another. Why *had* he been here? Oh yeah. "He said something about knowing who I was and finding that useful."

"You've been made?" Liv cried out.

I shook my head. "I don't think so. I mean, he didn't really come right out and say that."

"That doesn't mean it isn't true!"

"I know. He said something about us having a connection in common."

"What does that mean?" Liv looked alarmed.

"I don't know! I don't understand any of it!" I shouted.

"Maybe the Council set it up to make the job easier for you?" Liv said quietly.

Why didn't I think of that? Maybe that's what had happened. The Council somehow lured him to me. That had to be it!

"I'll buy that."

Liv frowned. "It has to be the answer. I can't think of any other reason." She pulled the stitches off my circular needles and sighed. "I really liked this scarf." Liv frogged it until it was completely unraveled. She then shredded the yarn into a pile of threads and we took them out to the patio and burned them.

It seemed to me like the yarn was a metaphor for my relationship, or soon to be lack thereof, with Diego. Either that or I was getting drunk at 10:15 a.m. Not good either way.

CHAPTER SEVENTEEN

"Wanna know the secret to winning? Creative sportsmanship. In other words, one has to rig the game."
—Agent Sands, *Once Upon a Time in Mexico*

I was having this really weird dream where Vivian Marcy could talk to tuna fish sandwiches and Diego was a mad scientist and I was a giant rutabaga, when the phone rang.

Caller ID said, "Dakota Bombay."

"Yes?" I croaked into the phone.

"Check the news on channel eight," my brother said before hanging up.

I sat up, reached for the remote to the TV and clicked it on.

"The victim, whose face and neck were mauled beyond recognition"—that woke me up—"was found in the tiger's exhibit at the zoo. The police have no idea who he is, how he got there or how he died." The reporter went on about similar cases at other zoos where drunks tried to climb in with animals only to be found dead the

next morning. She made some reference
to bestiality, but I shut off the TV.

The zoo? Wow. Dak had never been that
creative before. Usually, he ditched the
corpse and ran. But if the head and neck
were mauled, chances were they wouldn't
find out he'd been strangled. What the
hell did Dak do? Smear Vic's head with
A1 sauce?

The phone rang again. This time it was
Liv. "Impressive." She giggled. "He called
me too. Apparently, he's pretty proud of it."

I sighed with relief more than anything
else. "Looks like it'll be hard to trace."
We talked for a few minutes more before
realizing we had to get the kids to school.

Today was the big trip. Everything was
packed. It would just be a matter of getting
to the island. But I had another problem.

I'd planned to call Diego and let him
know I was going out of town. But how
could I do that when he had his hands full
with a missing client who was currently
resting, partially digested, in a tiger's
stomach?

After taking Romi to school, I cowboyed
up and called him. The phone rang five
times before going into voice mail.

"Diego?" *Of course, idiot! Who else
would it be*? I was so bad at leaving voice
messages. "It's Gin. I have to go out of
town for a few days to a family reunion.
I'll call you when I get back." I left my cell

phone number and hung up with a sigh of relief. There was a little tug at my stomach when I realized that I would really miss him.

Shit, Gin, what are you going to do when he leaves town for good? After all, you took out the only reason he had to be here!

The strange side of me who answers when I talk to myself was right. In making my family happy, I had screwed myself. Well, that was nothing new. Besides, it was a bad idea to get involved with a bodyguard.

There was that twinge again. Apparently, I had allowed myself to get more involved with him than I thought. It would be so easy to fall in love with Diego. But that couldn't happen. I needed to find a relationship with a clueless guy. Maybe someone who would be more into sports or NASCAR than worring about what I did for a living.

The twinge ignited into a fireball as I realized I didn't want anyone else. What was going on here? Was I falling for Diego? I picked up the phone and called again.

"Diego, it's Gin." Stupid voice mail. "Let's plan to get together as soon as I return from the reunion. I'll call you."

Now I sounded like a stalker. And while that's acceptable behavior for my job, I'm

pretty sure it doesn't work too well with
relationships.

Throughout the day, as I deposited
Poppy at Dad's, picked up a few more
things for the trip and prepared to pick
up Romi, all I could think about was
Diego. It would appear that I was already
starting to fall for him. Great.

At 3 p.m., Liv and I picked up the girls
from school and drove straight to the airport. We chatted about our trip during
the flight. Alta and Romi were thrilled.
They loved flying. It was fun watching
them crammed together, fogging up the
little window. Once we arrived at LAX, we
retrieved our bags and found our way to
the private hangar that housed the Bombay jet.

I breathed a sigh of relief when I saw we
were the only ones on the manifest.

"Hey, Joey," I called out to our pilot.

Joey nodded his reply and continued
checking everything in the cockpit. He
was a nice guy, in his sixties. Joey was the
family's full-time pilot. Which meant he
got paid a lot of money to make just a few
flights a year. He never asked questions
and was as silent as a rock. Good man.

Liv and I got the girls strapped into
their seats and were working on our own
seat belts when Joey came back.

"We're leaving. Got everything?" was

all he said. He was a man of very few words.

Liv and I nodded, and in a few minutes we were heading down the runway toward Santa Muerta . . . and far away from Diego.

CHAPTER EIGHTEEN

"Yes. The final supreme idiocy. Coming here to hide. The deserter hiding out in the middle of a battlefield."
—Lee, *The Magnificent Seven*

Santa Muerta. Yes, I knew it meant "Saint Death." Ironically enough, we didn't name it. Legend has it that in the eighteenth century, an English ship crashed on the rocks, shipwrecking thirty-three sailors. No one ever came to rescue them. The captain kept a log of their "visit." The screeching monkeys, complete lack of women and rum, and the burly first mate's penchant for bestiality (not with the monkeys, I'll bet), and they started to kill each other off, a la Agatha Christie meets the Donner Party. While Captain Smythe only hinted at the murderous motives, he described each murder until his own (of course) in grisly detail.

A few years later, I guess some Portuguese sailors found the shipwreck and investigated. All they found were thirty-two skulls stacked like a canned-goods display and the captain's logbook. They traveled to the mainland and explained what had happened to the fishermen there. The natives dubbed the island Santa Muerta.

Originally, the Bombays met at private residences. But after a few millennia of this, everyone was too nervous about "having the family over," so they bought this island.

My Great Aunt Dela(ware) and her daughter Cali(fornia) and granddaughter Missi(ssippi) live on Santa Muerta year-round. This is to maintain control over our hideaway. They employ twenty non-English–speaking natives, who actually run the place. Over the years, Dela and Cali have really turned the island into something nice.

If you visited Santa Muerta, you'd think you had landed at a Beaches Resort. (Of course, you'd be killed on the spot for trespassing, so your joy would be rather short-lived.) White sand surrounds the perimeter of a large jungle.

In the center is the main house. Well, it's more like a mansion, really, with forty guest rooms, a large meeting room with comfy, tiered seating and the latest multimedia presentation stuff, a ball-

room for parties, and an outdoor court-
yard with swimming pool complete with
cabana boys.

The manse sits beside a beautiful fresh-
water lake. Beyond the lake is a small
range of mountains with a high- and low-
ropes course for team-building exercises.
I am *not* kidding. We have to do this every
reunion. Try to picture thirty-five professional killers, ranging in age from five to
eighty-five, trying to do a "trust" fall
backwards into the arms of the *last*
group of people on earth you would trust.

To the north of the mansion is the
airstrip and dock. To the south are the
private bungalows. There are five of them,
more like luxury homes than rustic cab-
ins. These buildings are hidden in the
tree line, just off the beach.

The only rules on the island were not to
give the staff any information on who we
are or what we really do. (Seriously—you
think it's hard to find good help now? Try
it when the maids know you might kill
them if the sheets aren't soft enough.)
And at four p.m. every day, we have to be
inside one of the buildings until five.
Why? Because that's when the various
government satellites are overhead, taking
pictures.

Liv and I checked in at the airstrip, and
Paco (a.k.a. yummy cabana boy) took us
by Jeep to the house. By the way, since

women are in charge of the island, they hire the most gorgeous men to work there. All of us speak Spanish, so we made small talk until we arrived at the house. Paco winked at me as he carried our bags to the rooms.

"Mommy! I love this place!" Romi shrieked. Alta joined her and they raced around the lobby to check things out.

"Hey! There's a pool!" Alta shouted and Romi ran over to her.

Liv and I couldn't help smiling. We loved Santa Muerta too. If we weren't so exhausted from all the travel, we'd probably jump into the pool fully clothed while Paco brought us margaritas.

"Nap time first," I answered.

"Noooooooooo!" they screamed in unison.

Liv nodded. "Girls, we've been traveling all day. We need to take a break. Then we'll swim."

Both girls crossed their skinny arms over their chests and sullenly followed us to our rooms. We didn't need keys because the room locks were configured to our fingerprints. I hated dragging around keys or worse, those stupid plastic cards.

Liv and I had adjoining rooms. We opened the door between them and the girls bounced around, exploring. I opened the balcony doors just in time for a small orange monkey to leap onto the rail and shriek at me. Romi and Alta stared at the creature until it howled and dove into the fauna.

Somehow, we managed to get the girls to sleep. (I believe we threatened them with one of the tarantulas on the patio. *What?*) I passed out almost immediately.

The phone rang, waking me from a deep sleep. For a moment, I forgot where I was. That is, until the toucan bird outside the window cawed, or did whatever the hell they do.

"Hello?" No caller ID on these phones. Why was that?

"Hello, Virginia." Grandma's deep voice was gruff, but she sounded happy to hear me.

"Hey, Grandma! What's up?" I managed.

"Why don't you and Liv bring your girls to my room for tea?"

"Um, okay. When's that?"

"Now. See you in five." And she hung up.

I shook Liv's shoulder. "Grandma beckons."

Liv pushed her thick dark hair from her eyes, looking amazing even after sleeping. I hated her.

We scrambled to wake the girls, brush our teeth and head up to the penthouse floor. The five Council members had their own penthouse in the building. Liv and I exchanged glances as I knocked on Grandma Mary's door.

The peephole darkened, and I rolled my eyes. We're on a secure island, surrounded by assassins, and Grandma had to check to see who was there. And you thought your family had trust issues.

The door opened and Grandma stood there with a broad smile and open arms. Alta and Romi rushed into her embrace, covering her wizened face with kisses. Liv and I each gave her a hug and kiss, then followed her into her rooms.

"*Adios*, Juan," Grandma said briskly, dismissing the young man setting up the tea service.

I plopped down into a chair and began buttering a scone. Liv was already gulping down tea. The girls, on the other hand, were too busy checking out all the souvenirs from Grandma's travels. Totem poles from Alaska, a couple of shrunken heads from New Guinea (I'd been meaning to ask her if she did them herself), masks and spears from Africa, a mantilla and bullfighter's cape from Spain, Celtic knots carved from stone, and for some reason, a stuffed armadillo from Texas. And those were just part of the bizarre collection.

"Well, girls." Grandma sat and helped herself to a biscuit. "Did you have a nice trip?"

We chattered about nothing really. Grandma always seemed so gruff with everyone, but she was really a sweetie on the inside. One of my favorite relatives, she was a tiny woman, with soft crêpe skin, long white hair rolled up in a chignon, and piercing blue eyes, wearing a caftan and acting like a typical grandmother. And family was the most important thing to her. But I knew her dedication ran even deeper. She was completely committed to the Bombay way of life. And as much as I loved her, that was a little scary.

"I suppose you're ready for the girls to take the oath?" she asked as if she wanted to know what their favorite movie was.

"I guess so. As ready as you can be for that sort of thing," I replied, watching the girls play.

Grandma nodded as if she understood. "Where's Woody?"

Liv smiled. "Oh, he's coming with Dad. They stopped at the Alamo on the way." She rolled her eyes. "You know how Dad is. San Antonio is practically a religious pilgrimage."

"Well, he did wear that damned coonskin cap for four years until it fell apart," Grandma said.

I smiled too. Uncle Pete(rsburg) and his grandson were very close. They spent one weekend a month together doing something worthy of a sweat lodge bonding ritual. I had to admit, it was nice being around family. Liv and I were the only ones to give Grandma great-grandchildren, and I think that made us special. Not that she didn't dote on our brothers too. She spoiled them rotten.

"It's nice to have some time with my girls before the reunion starts," Grandma said. "And don't worry, Romi and Alta will do just fine. I understand you two reserved the Charlotte Corday Bungalow?"

"Yeah," I started.

"Did you say 'yeah'?" Grandma frowned at me.

I sighed. "I mean yes." She was a stickler for grammar and would have made one terrifying (and lethal) English teacher. "But Grandma, I'm more interested in the reason for the reunion."

Her eyebrows arched before she answered. "What do you mean, Ginny? Of course it's because Romi and Alta are ready for the oath."

"Liar, liar, pants on fire," I responded. Liv frowned.

Grandma changed her tactics. "Now girls, you know I can't reveal anything else until the Council announces it."

Liv put on her best pouty face. "Please? Just give us a hint."

Grandma's eyes flickered for a second, almost undone by Liv's big brown eyes. "Sorry. You'll have to do better than that.

Your parents didn't even try to pry it out of me."

Just then, Alta, followed closely by Romi, tackled Grandma and she laughed as she tickled them into an eruption of giggles.

"Fine," I said. "Don't tell us. And we won't warn you when you retire and Mom's on the Council."

Grandma laughed. "Nice try. But the only way I'm going off the council is by dying. If I have a debilitating stroke, I've always got my cyanide pill."

I had no doubt she'd use it too. As far as I knew, no Bombay ever did time in a nursing home. Too risky.

Grandma looked at her watch, then frowned. "Speaking of the Council, I'd better go. We have a meeting in five."

And that was it. She stood and herded us out of her apartment, leaving me to wonder why she'd called us up in the first place. Were Liv or I in trouble? I shuddered and thought of something more pleasant, like screaming monkeys.

CHAPTER NINETEEN

Miss Winter: With your ideas, I'm surprised you're shocked at the thought of war.
Ivan Dragomiloff: Not at all. It's purely a matter of business. How can we charge our sort of prices with everybody happily killing each other for a shilling a day?
—The Assassination Bureau

Dela and Cali run the island and handle the occasional South American job. The most interesting member of that family is my cousin Missi. If Richie was my nemesis, then Missi was my favorite relative (except for Liv, of course).

You know those wacky people you come across every now and then? The really colorful kind who don't care what others think? That was Missi. A little older than me, but also widowed with two sons, Missi cracked me up.

I'm sure you've seen the James Bond movies, the ones with Q, who's the inventor of 007's lethal gadgets. Missi is our Q. When she wasn't using poison frog darts on a Peruvian terrorist or some corrupt Colombian official, she was here at Santa

Muerta, coming up with some really cool stuff.

Let's see, what had she come up with that I could tell you about? Well, there was the special car bomb that ignited through the cigarette lighter. That had been cool because the authorities didn't catch it, and a major auto manufacturer recalled 100,000 cars thinking the explosion was their fault. One of my favorites was the remote-control icicle release mechanism. It might not sound like much, but she could actually create, then release, lethal icicles into the unsuspecting skull of a target. All the police would find was a wet spot. Brilliant!

"Monkeypops," I said into the small speaker outside Missi's workshop. The door sprang open and in I went. Did I mention her love of unusual passwords?

"Ginny!" Missi rose from her seat to hug me. Her magnifying goggles were still on her face, giving her a weird, eye-bulging effect.

"How are you? And Monty and Jack?" I asked.

"Hell as usual. Monty made his first kill last week." She moved to wipe away a nostalgic tear. "I can't believe it."

"They're fifteen already?" I couldn't believe it either. Had it been that long since I'd seen her?

Missi nodded, then pushed a stool toward me. I sat, and we caught up on what was going on.

Her workshop was one of my favorite places on earth. Unlike my sterile place, Missi filled every inch with really weird stuff. Sometimes I thought she spent her free time Dumpster diving in Chile. But everything there made sense to her. I guess that was what counted.

"So what's new?" I asked, hardly able to contain myself.

She smiled slowly. "What do you want?"

"You wouldn't happen to have any harmless nerve agent," (that I could use on, say, a Girl Scout troop?) "or something like that?"

Missi rolled her eyes. "Harmless? Hello! Assassin." She looked around the room. "Mostly I've been working on stuff for the new line."

My eyebrows shot up. "New line?"

She nodded. "The Council's asked me to look into another avenue of work for the family. It could be more lucrative."

"What are you talking about? We kill people. Or are we going to sell Amway now?"

"Actually, nothing as horrible as that. I'm working on some tech stuff to develop character assassination."

"You're joking."

"Nope," she replied, "and I think it's gonna be big. Probably a fate worse than death, if you think about it."

"Huh." But you know what? Living with a horrible scandal and spending the rest of your life being punished for a crime actually did sound worse.

"The Council's really excited about it."

I sat up. "Hey! Is that why we're meeting so early?" Yay! That was it! No one . . . well, in the family, anyway . . . bites it!

"No. That's not it." Missi shot me down. "We're about two years away from getting everyone started with this."

I folded my arms over my chest. "Well, then what the hell is going on?"

"I don't know," Missi said, looking wistful. "No one tells me anything. It's always, 'Missi, can you come up with a hairdryer to incinerate my hit?' or 'I need another contact lens case that shoots the poisonous needles into the eyes.' They only come to me when they want something."

"You made a hairdryer that incinerates the user?" I was stunned. This family needed a newsletter or something because that was way cool.

Missi waved me off. "It was nothing. You just have to get the heat right."

I sighed. "All right, so you don't know anything."

She grinned at me. "Nope. But I do have a surprise for you." She crooked her finger and rose from her stool. I followed her out into the garden to a patch of lilies. My love of botany made me giddy with expectation.

"There they are!" She pointed proudly. The white lilies were gorgeous, but what was the deal?

"I've seen white lilies before. What can they do?"

She actually rolled her eyes at me. "Not like these, you haven't. I don't have to tell you how plants take carbon dioxide from the air and turn it into oxygen."

Now I rolled my eyes. "Duh."

"Well, this will give FTD a run for its money. These babies do the reverse. They emit a gas to stun the Vic, then suck oxygen from the air and turn it into carbon dioxide."

I felt like she'd slapped me. "Are you serious?"

She nodded proudly. "I've been working on it for years. I've managed to come up with the perfect hybrid. All you do is pot several of these together and deliver them. Of course, they have to be inside to work effectively."

My excitement waned a bit. "So, how do you know they'll work?"

She put her hands on her hips. "Honestly, Gin! I tried it! It can take out a man in a small apartment in a couple of days."

I wasn't sure I wanted to know who she

tried it on, but I was really thrilled over this. Unfortunately, it would never make *Botany Today Magazine* for, well, obvious reasons. Missi's genius would once more go unrecognized by the rest of the world.

"Can we send some of these to Richie's room?" I asked, only slightly joking.

"I wish," Missi said, "but I don't want him to know I even have this stuff." She shuddered. "In fact, I always hope he forgets I'm here. That dumb-ass takes credit for my gadgets. Remember the personal groomer debacle?"

Did I ever. Missi had created a nose-hair trimmer that when activated, fired a laser into the victim's skull via the nasal passages. Richie told the Council he invented it. Only he set the frequency too high and it blew Vic's head clean off. When he learned the Council was pissed about it, he recanted and pointed the finger at Missi. See? I wasn't the only one who hated the son of a bitch.

I looked around. "You're still working on the Richinator, right?"

Missi nodded and grinned. Her dream invention would take Richie out completely during a hit. There were hundreds of prototypes, but nothing satisfactory yet. I *lived* for that day.

"Have you seen him yet?"

"No. Hey! Maybe he won't come and I can hunt him down or something."

Missi shot me a look. "Do you really want to get that close to him?"

We laughed and spent another hour talking about work. When I left her workshop, I had this renewed sense of purpose. Missi always motivated me.

"Family meeting at four," Liv told me as I walked into our rooms.

"Already?" I shouldn't have been surprised. After all, they always did this. First comes registration and an icebreaker, then keynote dinner and chocolate reception. At least we didn't have to wear name tags.

Tomorrow would be our individual evaluations with the Council, and the last day would be all about the rituals. Alta and Romi would have a sitter tonight—kids were excluded because they were usually bored to death. They would be involved in the ritual, then Liv and I would have our bungalow slumber party and we'd all go home.

At three-thirty, Luis arrived to baby-sit, and Liv and I went down to the conference center to check in. Mom and Uncle Pete were running the registration table. That meant Dak and Woody were around somewhere.

"Dad!" Liv called out. "Where's Woody?"

Uncle Pete winked at her. "Dak took him up to your room. We just got in, and Mom stuck us with this job."

My mother looked less enthusiastic. "I think we did this last time too." She handed me a large brown envelope. "Ginny, your meeting time with the Council is nine a.m. tomorrow. You won't be late, will you?" Her eyes were full of worry.

"Mom! I'm almost forty! Quit treating me like a kid!" I spun on my heel and walked away. You might think this was some big act of defiance, but in reality, we went through this ritual once a week.

"You know what?" Liv said once we were settled in our seats in the auditorium. We always tried to sit in the back. Actually, everyone tried to sit in the back. No one wanted anyone behind them in this room. "It feels like we were just here."

I rolled my eyes. "It's only been a year since the last meeting."

Liv looked at me for a moment. "That must be it."

The room filled up quickly, with most of my relatives sitting near immediate family. Mom, Pete, Dak and Paris slipped into the seats we'd been saving for them.

The Council assembled on the stage at a long table. Grandma was flanked by Lou on the left and Dela on the right. Her cousins, Troy and Florence, represented the European branch of the family and sat farther down. All I could think was that they looked old.

I wondered how long it would be before Mom and Pete joined their cousins to form the Council. Now that would be creepy. I'm not going to let Mom slide with any of that Council secrecy bullshit either.

Everyone in the room stood up to identify themselves, but we knew everybody already. Then came announcements. No icebreaker—which I was happy with because it was idiotic, and there was an announcement that the ropes course was being repaired. *Hey! I might actually enjoy this trip!* Once again we were reminded to go inside from four p.m. to five p.m. every day to avoid the satellites. Blah, blah, blah.

The one thing missing from the announcements was why the hell we were all here. Uncle Lou stood and dismissed us to the dining room for dinner. Sounded like a normal business conference, didn't it? It was, right down to the rubber chicken on the plate in front of me.

Liv munched on her vegetarian lasagna and we settled into a simple conversation of pleasantries with the family. Mom, Pete, Liv, me, Dak and Paris—your average family of assassins at an average family reunion.

CHAPTER TWENTY

Tom Stall: *In this family, we do not solve problems by hitting people!*
Jack Stall: *No, in this family we shoot them!*
—*A History of Violence*

Grandma stepped up to the microphone to start the keynote. Unlike normal conferences or conventions where you have an interesting speaker from outside the organization, our speaker was almost always a member of the Council. And they were all awful speakers. I groaned inwardly.

"Family is the most important thing we have," Grandma began. I started to tune out until her words sounded like the adults on Charlie Brown cartoons.

Instead, I focused on the tables around me. Actually, there weren't that many, only four in fact. And we were dead center.

To our right was Uncle Lou's family, with Mom's cousins York and Georgia and their kids, Sydney, Coney (Island) and Rich(mond)ie. Sydney's son, Clinton, and daughter, Savannah, were adults now, just starting their careers. Richie hadn't procreated (or wasn't allowed to).

On our left was Dela's family, with Cali, Missi, and Missi's twin sons, Monty and Jack. They sat with Cali's brother, Montana, and his unmarried children Lon(don) and Phil(adelphia). They reminded me of Mr. Wint and Mr. Kidd, the gay assassins from the James Bond flick *Diamonds Are Forever*.

The last table had the Europeans. Troy's daughter, Burma; her daughter, India; and granddaughter, Delhi (who was fifteen and would be making her first hit soon). Flo's daughter, Asia; granddaughter, Holland; and nineteen-year-old great-granddaughter, Madrid, joined them.

The European branch of the family only ever had one child each. I didn't know why that was, but it didn't really matter. I liked them. They seemed so mature. Or maybe it was just the accents.

Actually, I liked pretty much everyone. When we'd been in college, Liv and I would visit other family members during the summer breaks. Our brothers, Dakota and Paris, usually spent more time with the Europeans—especially at the family chalet in Switzerland. They skied constantly, always with new Scandinavian girls on their arms. And everyone doted on them. Bastards.

Grandma was onstage, wrapping up her

speech. I should've been a little ashamed that I didn't hear it, but from the looks on my family's faces, it was a real yawner.

The chocolate reception was the only thing I liked about these reunions. Every possible use you could think of for chocolate was there. And everything was in theme.

For instance, there were chocolate licorice garrotes, milk chocolate handguns, white chocolate asps, M & M's with skulls and crossbones on them, dark chocolate stilettos (and I don't mean shoes) and chocolate mousse "poisons" in edible glass candy test tubes. And milk. Lots of milk. That was the best part. Who can drink anything but milk with chocolate?

Anyway, I was at the fondue table drowning sponge cake bodies in the melted chocolate, when someone tapped me on the shoulder.

"Hey, Gin," Richie's asthmatic voice wheezed.

I ignored him.

The finger tapped harder, probably leaving bruises. "Gin!"

I turned with a sigh. I had to get this over with. "Oh, hi, Richie."

"So how are ya?" he asked with a slimy smile. Just looking at him made me lose my appetite. I should've killed him just for that.

"Just fine. How about you?" I had to force these words through my teeth.

Richie shrugged. "I'm training to be a ninja. Took out four guys last month."

This was all bullshit. He had to know I knew that. "Really? Were you supposed to do that?" I asked innocently.

Richie's fat cheeks flamed red. "Yes. I was. The Council knows I can handle it and so they've been stepping up the assignments." He started to cool down, waving his hand nonchalantly. "And the ninja thing is mainly for the chicks."

Now I wanted to vomit. "Is that right?" I managed.

He nodded. "Well, I've always had a natural talent with the martial arts," he paused dramatically, "and with the ladies."

I started to laugh and milk came out of my nose. I assumed when he said "ladies," he meant the latex, blow-up kind.

"I suppose I should settle down someday," he mused, ignoring my giggle fit. "But it really wouldn't be fair to just choose one woman."

I guffawed. I wanted to say something very sarcastic about his so-called way with women, but instead I shoved two or three pieces of cake victims in my mouth to stop myself. Of course, this caused me to choke violently.

Before I knew what was happening,

Richie yelped, "I'll save you!" The son-of-a-bitch wrapped his arms around me, trying to crush my ribs to get the food out. I couldn't breathe, but I was thinking nothing could be worse than having that dumb-ass save my life.

The food remained lodged in my windpipe as Richie squeezed me again and again. He wasn't doing it right, and I had the feeling I was turning blue. I brought my arms up, forcing Richie to release me and threw myself onto my own fist on the back of the chair. The pressure on my sternum popped the slimy chunk of cake out of my mouth and I slipped to the floor.

"You saved her, Richie!" "You're a hero, boy!" Voices praised Richie all around me and I thought, *That's it. I've died and gone to hell.*

No such luck. Apparently, no one saw me save myself. Everyone in the whole goddamned family thought Richie saved me. It was my worst nightmare come true. Now I *really* wanted to kill him.

"Gin was eating so fast, stuffing it in like a pig." Richie's voice floated down to the floor where I lay. "I tried to stop her, but it's obvious she has an eating problem. I'd say she's put on thirty pounds since last year."

It's just twenty pounds, you moron! I struggled to get to my feet and looked at the room of amazed family members. Liv and Dak grabbed my arms and dragged me out of the room.

"Let me go!" I fought them. "I have to go in there and kill him!"

But Liv and Dak wouldn't give up until I was outside by the pool.

"What were you thinking in there?" Dak asked incredulously.

"Nothing! I just crammed food into my mouth so I wouldn't say anything stupid!" I protested weakly.

"Well, now you've made him a hero!" Liv cried out.

"He didn't save me! I did!" I yelled.

Dak and Liv studied me for a moment, then exchanged arched eyebrows with each other. Great. They thought Richie really did save me. Hell, the whole Bombay family thought that!

"Focus!" Liv snapped.

I took a deep breath. "Okay. Give me a reason why I shouldn't go back in there."

Dak grinned. "We know Richie didn't do anything. Probably everyone else does too. He's not worth it, Gin."

Liv folded her arms across her chest and nodded in agreement.

"All right, then let's go to the bar. I need a triple."

"Triple what?" Liv asked.

"A triple anything."

*   *   *

Which is how I ended up at eight-thirty in the morning, gulping down coffee and feeling like I was dead. Great, my appointment with the Council was in half an hour and I was grotesquely hungover. My skin was clammy, and it felt like there were beetles crawling around underneath. Even my hair follicles hurt. If my family wasn't trying to kill me with humiliation, they were doing so with alcohol poisoning.

I made it to the Brutus Conference Room just in time.

"Sit down, Virginia, please," Grandma ordered. Lou, Dela, Troy and Florence all nodded.

The Council members sat in high, leather-backed seats on a platform in a semicircle around me. I sat in a simple leather chair below them, which meant psychologically I was at a disadvantage. The walls were dark with mahogany paneling. It would make a great room for a war tribunal.

Lou spoke up first. "Virginia, you have done very well with all of your assignments in the last year."

What? Praise from Lou? I was sure I had a shocked look on my face.

Troy added in his clipped English accent, "Especially your last two assignments. And while I think the methods were a bit . . ." He paused to think of the right word, "*extreme*, you managed it."

"My brother is understating what we all feel was a job well done," Florence said.

I sat up a little straighter in my chair. But I said nothing. You weren't allowed to speak until the Council invited you to.

Dela spoke next and I wondered if they'd all rehearsed taking turns. "Which is why this isn't an ordinary evaluation."

Troy frowned at her, before turning to me. "I'm sure you have wondered why the reunion is taking place so soon. It is because we have a rather serious dilemma and we need you to take care of it."

My mouth dropped open at that point, only adding to my look of hungover moron. But I still didn't speak—even though I damn well wanted to. They needed my help?

Grandma folded her hands. "The last two jobs were tests, Ginny. We wanted to see how you could handle the stress. The real job is what you are here for." She waved her arms around her. "What we are all here for."

There was a pause, and for a moment, I opened my mouth, then closed it. The Council was going to tell me what the job was, right? Or were we going to play charades? And let me tell you, I sucked at charades.

"There is a mole in the family," Lou said. "We need you to find out who it is and take care of it."

Okay, now I was stunned. It was hard enough to get over the compliment-palooza earlier, but a mole? In our family? Who'd be that stupid?

"We've learned through our sources," Dela explained, "that one of the Bombays has been providing information to the FBI and Scotland Yard. We don't believe at this time that the information is damaging, but we want it stopped."

Well, duh! Can I talk now?

"We are trusting you to find out who the traitor is and dispatch them," Troy said. "Any questions?"

"Yeah!" I shouted, earning a stern look from Grandma. "I mean, yes. I have several. First, are you convinced it's blooded family?" The Council nodded (rather creepily) in unison. "Okay, how do you know that? What do you have? What information will you give me? What is my timeline? Do I really have to kill them, or do I just turn them over to you?" Actually, it would be a more merciful death if I just killed whoever it was.

Lou held up his hand. "I know this is a tough assignment. I once had to take out a family member, as you well know. But it's the way we do things. It's what has made our enterprise successful all these thousands of years."

"No one else here will know what we've told you," Grandma said. "We are announcing that it has to do with the children who have reached ritual age. You are, under no circumstances, to talk to anyone about this." She waved her finger at me. "Not your mother. Not your brother or your cousin. No one."

Troy made a face. "It could even be one of them, Virginia. That is why we must tread lightly."

I really, really wanted to roll my eyes.

Grandma slapped the table, startling me. "I mean it! Tell no one!"

Dang, she was touchy. Well, I guess she did watch her brother kill her daughter. Okay, fine. Geez.

"Dela will be your contact," Lou added. "You'll meet with her tonight at five p.m. in her room. Don't talk about that either."

Flo smiled, trying to lighten the situation. "Just tell everyone we are pleased with your work. Dela will be your handler in all matters relating to this. Any other questions?"

"Yea . . . I mean yes. Why only Dela?" I had many more questions but this one popped out first.

Troy glared. "Because it will be easier for you and for us. This way we know the situation is being handled competently and you only need to go to one person to report."

A rap at the door told me my evaluation was over. Someone else waited outside. I rose and nodded to the Council, letting myself out.

Richie sneered at me on his way in. I smiled back because he might be the mole. *Well, he could be, right?*

CHAPTER TWENTY-ONE

"No matter how many times you save the world, it always manages to get back in jeopardy again. Sometimes I just want it to stay saved! You know, for a little bit? I feel like the maid; I just cleaned up this mess! Can we keep it clean for . . . for ten minutes?"
—Mr. Incredible, *The Incredibles*

A mole. In the Bombay family. I kid you not—these were the two sentences that went through my mind over and over again as I sat by the pool, watching Liv and Dak play with the kids. I told everyone I got a good review, but they seemed doubtful. Gee, maybe it was the cartoon thundercloud over my head, or the fact I only responded in monosyllabic grunts.

Okay, so I wasn't much of an actress. I twirled my straw in the lemonade Paco brought me. He kept asking if I wanted something stronger in it, but I said no. The hangover was long forgotten, but worry had set in. And I needed to be sober to meet with Dela.

My eyes searched the pool, scanning every family member nearby. One of these thirty-five people was ratting out the family. Again I thought of Richie, but then realized I had to be more practical. The only things that condemned him were (1) he was an idiot, and (2) I wanted it to be him.

I cleared my throat in hopes of clearing my thoughts. No. This was serious. And it wasn't going to be easy. Even though I fantasized that Aunt Dela would give me a complete dossier with the traitor's photo and schedule for the next week, I knew better. If they had even the slightest idea who it was, that person would be made an example of at the reunion. Not good.

So I would have to find out who it was. But how? I wasn't a detective. I guess the only good thing about this was that the Council felt certain it wasn't me. I was not a suspect. Well, that and the fact that I knew I wasn't talking to the Feds. And I knew it couldn't be Mom, Dak or Liv. Okay. That's four people out of thirty-five. Only thirty-one more suspects to go.

What was the first thing to look at? I thought about all those Agatha Christie novels I had read in high school. Now, what was that "m" word thingy that every murderer had to have? Motion . . . motor . . . motel . . . motive! That's it! If I could figure out the motivation behind the treason, I might be able to find the fink.

I shifted in my rattan seat, causing my sunglasses to slip to the end of my nose.

I pushed them back up. Somehow, they felt like protection. A barrier between me and disaster.

What would it take to betray the family? Money was out. We were all filthy rich. And it wasn't like the government could tempt us with more than we already had. Maybe the mole got caught? Perhaps it was some kind of blackmail?

In spite of the hot weather, I shivered. The entire Bombay family could be put in prison for the things we'd done. And right or wrong, what we'd been doing for millennia (although I was pretty sure the statute of limitations had run out on historical assassinations) really boiled down to murder, plain and simple. Shit.

If it was blackmail, then we were all in danger. Hell, if the Scotland Yard was involved, the European branch was in trouble too. I felt my frown lines deepen. Wouldn't that be ironic? The government imprisoning assassins they hired regularly? Of course, I wasn't supposed to know about that, but I'm not an idiot.

Okay, blackmail was bad. It meant the mole could be anyone. Not good. How about revenge? No, that wouldn't be it. Anyone implicating the family would turn up implicated as well. That left stupidity.

Stupidity as a motive was highly underrated in this family. Look at Richie. I shook my head, looking a little insane to those around me. I couldn't count on it being Richie. But who else could it be?

I spent the rest of the day like this, excusing myself as hungover. At four-thirty I showered and dressed, and at five, I knocked on Dela's door.

"Come in, Gin!" I heard the door locks pop and went into the penthouse. I'd never been in Dela's rooms before. Oooh. She was a wicker chick. Every piece of furniture was wicker or rattan. Large ceiling fans hung in each room, lazily spinning the humid air about. Tropical potted plants and a tiled floor made me feel like I was in Mexico. And in a bizarre twist, every wall was covered with paintings of matadors on black velvet.

"Sit down," Dela said, directing me to a table laid out with dinner for two. "We're eating in here tonight."

The enchiladas and fried plantains made my mouth water. I joined her at the table and began to eat, waiting for her to speak first.

She waited until we were done with our first glass of wine. A Chilean shiraz, I think.

"So what do you think of our little problem?"

Little problem? "Um, well, I don't know yet," I responded brilliantly.

Dela nodded. "Of course you don't. And

I'll bet you were hoping I would have a complete dossier, right?"

I swallowed my wine before answering. "That's right. But I'm guessing that's not the case."

"No. I don't have much to give you, in fact."

"So how do you know about the FBI and the Yard?" I asked.

Dela sighed. "For years we've had connections in certain government departments. Our contacts tipped us off just recently."

"I suppose Interpol and the CIA are next?" All right, I probably didn't have to be such a smartass about it.

"No, they aren't involved. But the agencies that are could jeopardize our family."

That part, I'd guessed. "What have our contacts told us?"

Dela poured me another glass of wine. "Please understand, Gin, our contacts are just as upset as we are."

I rolled my eyes. "Oh sure. But they won't go to prison, now, will they? Or have their entire family put away? No, that risk is exclusively ours."

Dela frowned. "I understand that you're upset and am pleased you are concerned about the family's interests. . . ."

"I don't give a damn about the family's interests but I do care a lot about the family members."

"Okay. Fine, "Dela said." I agree with that. But let me tell you that the risk is minor right now. The mole has only promised information, but hasn't yet delivered it yet."

"What are they asking for? What's the motivation?"

Dela leaned back. "I don't know. The only thing we can rule out is blackmail. Apparently the mole is not under suspicion."

"Do we know if it's male or female? Do we have anything to go on whatsoever?" My voice got louder.

"I know you're upset, Gin. But don't take it out on me. I volunteered to be your handler. Just think how Lou, Troy or your own grandmother would take your attitude."

She had me there. I was behaving badly. "Sorry. I'm just a little freaked out."

"I know. We are too. This isn't an easy or pleasant assignment. But that's why we picked you."

"Because I'm difficult? Or unpleasant?" I smiled.

Dela laughed. "Both. But also because you're one of our sharpest employees."

I winced at her words. I never thought of myself as anything more than bungling. And calling me an employee instead of a member of the family was weird too.

"So where do we start?" I asked, polishing off another glass of wine.

"Well, we know it's someone in your generation. Both contacts describe the individual as male. They refused to give us more information, perhaps because it's too sensitive, or maybe they don't know anything else."

"A young male? Well, that does narrow it down somewhat." I ticked them off on my fingers: "Coney, Richie, Lon and Phil."

"And Dak and Paris," Dela added.

I shook my head. "No way. Dak and Paris wouldn't do anything that stupid."

"It doesn't matter what you think, Gin. Dak and Paris are to be investigated just as vigorously as the others."

"Yeah," I said, "but I know neither of them are the mole."

"Do you?" Dela's blue eyes went cold and I realized that even though I felt confident of Dak's and Paris's innocence, the Council did not.

"Fine. Just to make you happy, I'll look into them too."

"This is very serious, Gin. You have to treat all six men as equal suspects, or this won't work."

"Sorry. I will." But I knew Dak and Paris weren't involved. Meaning I really had only four suspects. "What else can you tell me?"

"Only that you have two weeks to find and take care of him."

"That's it? Two weeks? Fourteen days? That's all I have?" I protested.

"In two weeks, the snitch is meeting with his contacts from both agencies at the same time. We need to neutralize the problem before that meeting happens."

"Wait, you know that much, but you don't know who it is or why he's doing it?"

She nodded. "We even know the meeting will take place at a Starbucks in Washington, D.C., at five p.m. But we don't know who it is."

I loved Starbucks. I really did. I even took offense when comedians make fun of them. For one of my cousins to besmirch the company's name for a Bombay family takedown was over the top, in my humble opinion.

"Since I know it's a male, does that mean I can enlist help from my female cousins?" Liv was smarter than I was. I'd bet she could have the info to the Council in one week.

"Absolutely not. If you're talking about Liv, her brother is a suspect, don't forget. Even your mother isn't to know because of Dak."

"So why didn't you use one of the female cousins who don't have brothers for this job?"

Dela narrowed her eyes at me. "Because we wanted you. Remember, under

no circumstances are you to involve anyone else. Especially Liv."

"Is this a joke?" Liv's big brown eyes
pleaded with me two hours later when I,
of course, told her everything. Hey, I
wasn't smart enough to do this alone.
Sue me.

CHAPTER TWENTY-TWO

*"I've decided what I want to do with
my life. I wanna be a cleaner."*
—Mathilda, *The Professional*

I waited a moment for the information to
sink in. I mean, it took me about twenty
hours. Of course my timing isn't perfect.
We were just getting ready to take the
girls down to the conference center for
their ritual. The way I saw it, Liv could
think about it for a while, and then when
we got to the bungalows we could discuss
it intelligently.

"I don't believe it!" Liv looked pretty upset. Maybe I had figured it wrong.

"Well, I don't believe it either. That is,
that Dak or Paris could be involved. I
mean, I definitely believe it about the
mole," I fumbled.

"We'll discuss this later!" she hissed
and I got the distinct impression she was
pissed off. Not good. Not now, at least.

An hour later, after the older kids went through their ceremonies, I felt my insides bunch up into my throat as Grandma (wearing a goat skull for some ungodly reason—I never did get that part of the ritual; frankly, I think she just liked wearing it.) called Romi and Alta to the front of the candlelit room.

"Now, we open our arms to the youngest members of the family," Grandma intoned dramatically. I couldn't help doing the old eye roll in Liv's direction. She shot me a fierce look that pierced my spleen. Okay, she was still pissed.

Romi and Alta looked doubtfully at Grandma, but nodded when she asked them if they were ready. Ready for what? To start killing people? To hunt down errant family members if necessary?

Romi looked back at me with a cocked eyebrow. My darling little cynic. She thought we'd all lost our minds. That was so cute! And they looked darling in their little white dresses.

Uncle Lou stepped forward, droning on and on about loyalty to family, blah, blah, blah. Then he asked them to hold out their arms.

Shit! I forgot to tell them about this part! Romi freaks out when she gets a shot. Liv grabbed my hand, and I realized she was thinking the same thing. I started thinking that it would be cool if we really had telepathic abilities. I bet we could really kick some ass. . . .

An angry shout brought my attention back where it belonged. Uncle Lou had drawn the ceremonial dagger (which, personally I think should have been replaced two millennia ago—I mean, seriously, we could get tetanus from that old thing!) across Romi's palm, drawing blood. And my daughter responded by clocking him in the nose with a pretty impressive right cross. I couldn't help smiling.

I was about to go up there when Grandma pulled her aside, whispering something into her ear. Alta stood there stoically (or maybe she was in shock) as Lou did the same to her. Romi still looked angry as they were led to a table and signed their names to the family book in their own blood. Nice. Too bad Hallmark doesn't make a card to mark that sort of occasion.

"Mommy!" I heard Romi yell. "I do *not* like this!" My older relatives gasped in shock while I saw Dak smothering a grin. He flashed me the thumbs-up sign.

It was even worse when Grandma tried to get them to wipe their bloodstained hands on their snow white gowns. It was part of the thing. Innocence lost—crap like that. Unfortunately for her, the girls fought hard. Ruining a "princess dress," as they had called it earlier that evening, was out of the question. Romi kicked Grandma in the shins while Alta ran in evasive zig-zag maneuvers. It was pretty funny. Even Liv joined me in laughing, which was inappropriate, I guess.

Grandma and Lou gave up, finally, and our daughters, in their pristine gowns and completely disheveled hair, marched like queens back to us. Liv and I carefully bandaged their hands, but they only glared at us. Okay, so not preparing them for it was a bad idea. It was clearly going to be a very long night in the bungalow.

"I'm *never* going to forget this, Mommy!" Romi said for the fifteenth (or was it fiftieth?) time. She shoved a handful of popcorn into her mouth and chewed angrily (if that's possible).

"Yeah!" Alta added, looking mournfully at her bandaged hand.

"I told you, I'm sorry!" I said again, hoping it would sink in this time.

Alta glanced sideways at her mother. "Did you really do that when you were a kid?" Liv had tried empathy, pleading that the same thing had happened to her, Woody, even Grandpa Pete, but Alta didn't seem to believe it.

Okay, we blew it. All I could see was failure. Hell, I'd probably blow the sex talk in a few years too.

"Look," Liv pleaded, "it's getting late and we've had a long day."

I nodded. "Yes! Good idea! We can talk about it more tomorrow." Something in Romi's glare told me that it would be an unpleasant discussion. "At the beach," I added as a bribe.

The girls glared at us one more time, then curled up in their beds and closed their eyes. Liv and I waited until we were sure they were asleep, and we had a couple of beers. Then she asked me to tell her the whole mole story again. I tried to throw in a few dramatic flairs to make it seem more interesting, but my heart just wasn't in it.

"Well," she sniffed, "I think it's safe to assume that Dak and Paris are clear."

"I tried to tell Dela that. But she insists we investigate them just as thoroughly."

"And we only have two weeks?" Liv asked again.

I brightened. She said "we"! I nodded like a bobblehead doll.

"Well then, let's start with Dak and Paris so we can write them off immediately."

"Brilliant!" I opened another beer. "Then the Council will see that I did what I was asked. And don't forget, you know nothing about this."

She nodded. "But, Gin, two weeks isn't enough time to investigate one hit, let alone six men. Maybe they'll give you more time?"

I shook my head. "Sorry. The mole

squeals in a Starbucks to two different governments in two weeks. I have to have him hog-tied and bleeding before then." Why did I sound like an extra from *Deliverance*?

Liv opened another beer. "I guess we'll just have to get started immediately. How are we going to do this, by the way?"

I gaped. "I thought you knew! Hell, that's why I brought you into this mess!"

She shook her head. "I've had too much to drink and apologizing for the last two hours has given me a migraine. Let's work on it tomorrow."

"Another great idea! I knew filling you in was the right thing to do!" I slurred rather drunkenly. Yes! We would think about it tomorrow! *After all . . . tomorrow is another day!* And we don't even have to make clothes out of the drapes! Woo-hoo!

CHAPTER TWENTY-THREE

"Death is life's way of telling you you're fired."

—Author Unknown

You know, I was getting pretty drunk on this stupid island. But can you blame me? I had been "rescued" by the one person I loathed more than Vivian Marcy, given an impossible job by the Council (but they did give me a good evaluation, so I guess that counts for something), and watched my baby take the blood oath that would bind her to the Bombay merchant o' death machine and begin her training as an assassin.

It's funny how many people I met in college who were going into the "family business" after school. Some were proud to—others dreaded it. I never realized how much I was like them before now. Romi had just started her education last night, and I was going to be killing off one of my cousins soon.

Hell, I couldn't even get relationships right! I seriously doubted that anyone had killed off her lover's client and managed to make the relationship work. I hadn't heard from Diego. I didn't even know whether he had found out about his boss. For all I knew, he could've been on a flight back to Australia as I was thinking this!

Liv was in the shower and the girls were putting on their swimsuits. I slipped out of the bungalow and pulled out my cell phone.

"Diego Jones speaking." His voice was as rough and warm as good scotch.

"Gin?" asked the voice, "is that you?"

Shit. He had caller ID. "Um, hey, Diego. How's things?"

"I've been trying to call you." His voice sounded urgent, "The shit's hit the fan here. I lost my client." There was an awful pause. I knew it wasn't easy for him to admit that.

"Diego, I'm so sorry. What happened?" Like I didn't know.

"I'll tell you when you get back. We have a lot to talk about."

Uh oh. What did *that* mean? "Um, good. I'll be home tomorrow night. Why don't you come over the next day at nine, after I take Romi to school?" *So we can have sex and I can make you forget your terrorist-funding client, who, by the way, I happened to have killed.*

Liv stepped out onto the porch, her arms crossed over her chest, smiling at me.

"Sounds good," Diego said. "And Gin? I really miss you," he said before hanging up.

He missed me! I leaned against the doorway to keep from swooning.

"Lover Boy from Down Under doesn't connect you to the hit, does he?" Liv teased.

"God, I hope not. That might negatively impact our romance."

"Riiiiiiight."

The girls bounced out the door and down the steps to the beach. Liv and I scooped up the cooler and lounge chairs and followed their tiny footprints in the sand.

The girls, we discovered, were way more interested in chasing fiddler crabs and wading into the surf than in hearing from us about their future careers. Liv and I found an isolated shady spot and set up our stuff.

"So," I started, "I investigate our brothers first."

Liv looked at me over her sunglasses. "Actually, you should investigate Dak first."

I nodded. "Right. So how do I do that?"

Liv peered at the lame dossier Dela had given me. "I don't know."

"I could check on his whereabouts on the dates the mole met with the two agencies. How hard could that be? He never goes anywhere without telling me or Mom."

She nodded. "And he has no motive, really. Dak loves his playboy-with-a-trust-fund lifestyle. In fact, I'm curious what the motivation is at all."

"I'll check with him about those dates first. Then I'll hack into the bank's computer and confirm that his accounts haven't suddenly become larger. Do you think that will do?"

"I guess," she replied absently. "I mean, what else is there? You only have two weeks."

"You check out your brother. Gather the same evidence. That will save us some time. Oh! And we should search their homes too. That way, we can prove we had nothing to go on."

Liv sipped her margarita. "So who do you think it is?"

I leaned back. "I hope it's Richie. But it could be Lon and Phil. I'm sure it's not Coney."

"How can you know that?" Liv asked.

I shrugged. "I don't know. We've always gotten along, and I just don't see him doing that. Lon and Phil are weird, though."

"Yes they are, but that doesn't mean they would turn the whole family in."

"Well, why not?" I argued. "After all, they don't have wives or kids to worry about. If they get some kind of deal, it's only their mom who goes to prison."

"And their father, grandmother, and so on. I don't think we can count on that. Whoever the mole is, he obviously has selfish motives."

We sat there quietly for a moment, turning the idea over in our heads. And while I appreciated a good mind-bender like anyone else, I hated this.

"Well, let's just start on Paris and Dak and figure it out as we go," Liv finally said.

"Fine."

The day went very well as we sat there, watching the girls playing while we made small talk. Liv suggested I keep Diego at a distance . . . at least until this mole issue was taken care of.

And maybe she was right. Diego and I had issues that would take years of therapy to work out. And I wasn't so sure he was ready to become Diego Bombay. And at this point, I wasn't so sure I still wanted to be a Bombay. The girls were avoiding any conversation on last night's fiasco, and I had a sticky job to do.

I outlined in my head (while Liv napped in her chaise beside me) what I needed to do to get Dak off the hook when we got home. That made me feel a little better. Well, that and the fact that I would see Diego soon.

* * *

Later that afternoon, we went back to the manse. Liv and I had given up talking to the kids about the family. They formed a tiny but impenetrable wall of defiance we couldn't breach. I'd be lying if I said we weren't relieved to be failures.

After dinner, Liv and Dak took the kids to the pool while I slipped out to visit Missi again. I couldn't tell her what was up, but I had to see if she had any good surveillance stuff. And maybe I could get a little intel on her cousins Lon and Phil.

I came bearing kiwi daiquiris (Missi's favorite), and she seemed pleased to see me. I felt like I should whisper "I'm in" to some electronic device on my person.

"Surveillance equipment, eh?" Missi chewed on her lip. She turned and led me to a corner of her workshop. "I have the usual stuff, X-ray binoculars, mini-cameras hidden inside souvenir snow globes, Chia Pets with supersonic listening devices and . . ."

"Chia Pets?" I interrupted.

She shrugged. "Weird as it may sound, nearly everyone gets one as a gift at some point in their lives. Works really well too." She pointed at the photo on the box with the plants forming an Afro on the terra cotta head. "I've created plants where half the leaves are fiber optic microphones."

I wondered if my cousins would throw them away the minute I gave them out.

What reason would I have to send these guys Chia Pets anyway? I'd have Liv think about that one. She'd come up with some good reason.

"I'll take six." I said.

Missi grabbed a basket. "Any preferences? I've got everything from human heads, to hedgehogs, to Scooby Doo."

"Just give me one of everything." I had no idea what I was doing. When in doubt, always go with an assortment. That's what I always said. At least starting right now, that's what I always said.

"Oh! I've got a new phone tap that's really cool!" She grinned. I loved her enthusiasm.

"Has anyone else been by to utilize your talents? I mean, you are such an asset to the family, I can't imagine that no one else has raided your stash." I had to know that if I sent someone a Chia Pet, he wouldn't already have one.

"Not this trip. You're it. I think the others only come to me when they're stuck."

"Tell me about the phone taps." I held out my basket.

"It's some of my best work, really!" She handed me a small machine that looked suspiciously like an iPod. "You type in the phone numbers you want—up to six—and hit 'record.' Plug the thing that looks like a charger into your phone jack. The device works through the phone line and holds up to forty-eight hours for each phone. And it's a ten-gigabyte MP3 player too."

That was funny. I had six numbers to tap and it held six. What a coincidence. Missi showed me how to program the tap and threw in a purple ostrich-skin case and fifty free music downloads.

We were halfway through the cocktails when I decided to ask about her cousins.

"How's the family?" I hoped that sounded natural. The squeak in my voice might have given me away.

"Okay. Nothin' much going on." She ran down her immediate family. Ordinary stuff, but nothing about her cousins.

"I saw Lon and Phil this morning. I still can't tell them apart."

Missi laughed. "Yeah, those two are strange. Most twins want to be individuals. But those two try to find ways to look even more like each other."

"I'm close to my cousins Paris and Liv. Are you guys close?" Did that sound too obvious?"

She shook her head, "I don't see them very much. And they keep to themselves. They even live together, if you can believe that."

That was weird. But it would make my phone tap a lot easier.

"Any sign of girlfriends . . . or maybe boyfriends?" I was on eggshells here.

Missi cocked an eyebrow. "Nothing that I can see. They're probably androgynous." She shook her head. "No, I never really knew them. Even as kids they were a pair of loners. I think that's why they like living in New York City. Pretty anonymous there, I would think."

I sensed the conversation was over, so I thanked her for the gadgets and left. We were heading back tomorrow and I had to pack, pick up the latest edition of the family directory, get my complimentary family reunion photo and fill in Liv on my progress. But first, I had to download some killer tunes to my new toy.

CHAPTER TWENTY-FOUR

"Always read stuff that will make you look good if you die in the middle of it."

—P. J. O'Rourke

In every family, there's a black sheep. Someone who doesn't quite fit in. You might think that would be everyone in my family, but you'd be wrong. Other than having The Grim Reaper as a job title, most of us are fairly normal.

Well, not everyone. Our family's black sheep was Coney Bombay. I was always drawn to the stranger relatives. I didn't know why. Maybe it had something to do with the fact that we all had the same job—every last one of us. Not much interesting conversation when you were in a room full of people with the same occupation. Granted, this was the only place I could talk shop with a bunch of people. But dull nonetheless. Anyway, Coney, named for that trashy little island of

thrills in New York, is a carnival enter-
tainment technician.

Which means, you guessed it . . . Coney
was a carny. Actually, he prefered the
term carny. And did he dress the part.
Most people would avoid him because of
his shaved head, long beard and many
tattoos. But I was one of the few people
who knew he had a Ph.D. in philosophy.
So, why did he do the carnival thing?
Probably something in that brainy head
of his made it all even out in the end.
When I'd been younger, I thought he was
cool because he was rebelling against the
family. But I'd seen his tricked-out RV,
and he hadn't avoided the trust fund. His
transient lifestyle made it easier for the
wet work.

Coney was the same age as my brother,
and we actually got along great. The rest
of the family looked down their noses at
him, but he was really quite cool. If you
met him in a dark alley, even without
knowing what he did for a living, you'd be
scared. At six foot seven inches, with a
powerful frame, he was a big guy.

He favored muscle T-shirts, probably so
you could see the tattoos that covered
every inch of his arms, shoulders and
torso. But if you looked closer (and believe me, no one ever did) you would notice that each tattoo had a story steeped
in mythology or philosophy. Which would

lead to the tatty paperback book by John Stuart Mill or Ayn Rand or whoever he was reading at the time. Of course, his outward appearance usually dictated that no one would look closer.

I admired Coney. Why? I guess because he loved what he did. He actually liked stuffing sticky brats onto a thrill ride of questionable safety. And the gig was great for his cover. Since he lived out of an RV, there was no personal address. He lived pretty much off the grid. Unlike the rest of us who basically did things like other people—got married, had kids, and paid taxes—Coney had a freedom most of us only dream of.

I found him sitting by the pool when I got back from Missi's lab. It was dark, and he was the only one there, nose deep in a book by Jean-Paul Sartre . . . in French, no less. I flung myself down beside him. He looked up and smiled.

"Hey, Ginny." Coney looked like hell but smelled like that new very expensive Armani cologne.

"Hey, Coney!" I leaned over and hugged him, realizing how weird that would look in the real world.

"How're they hanging?"

I shook my head. "Don't try slumming it with me. I was there when you graduated magna cum laude from Yale."

"Sure, but right now I wish I were back in

my sweet RV in Florida." He threw his thumb over his shoulder. "I hate this crap."

"Me too. But it keeps you in your posh lifestyle and me from having to put Romi in day care."

Coney smiled, revealing two new gold embellishments on his teeth. "Oh, man. She was hilarious at the ritual. How're you handlin' that?"

"As well as any soccer mom could, I guess."

"Yeah, but how many soccer moms do you know who can poison a captain of industry and still make a mean Twinkie cake in time for the bake sale?"

"Are you teasing me?"

"Duh."

"Well, stop it or I'll send you a Twinkie cake that will give you diarrhea for a month."

He laughed, lightly punching me in the arm. "Okay, then let's switch subjects. How's the love life?"

"What love life?" I countered, feeling a little guilty for lying.

"Bullshit. Dak told me about the Australian."

"Remind me why we aren't allowed to kill members of the family again?"

"I don't know, but if anything changes, they'll find my brother Richie dead in a freak bumper car accident."

"I thought you handled the roller coaster."

Coney winked. "I got promoted."

"Well, cousin, you'll have to beat me to the punch on that hit."

"So what else's up?" It's amazing that someone who could read difficult French philosophers in their native tongue could have such a limited vocabulary.

"Not much. We're leaving tomorrow."

"Me too. Gotta show in Truckee."

I laughed. "I wish we could've had more time together. You know how much I love your stories."

Coney smiled and tucked a bookmark into his book. "Yeah. These reunions aren't very social, are they?"

"Nope. We're not even one of those families that gets together for weddings and funerals." And there weren't many of those, I might add. "Maybe we can grab a few beers when you head through the Midwest again?"

He scratched his beard. "Well, I guess I'll be in Peoria in a couple of months. You're in the directory, right?"

We both laughed at this. Coney was the one person with whom I could enjoy the irony about our family and its business.

"Somethin' botherin' you?" he asked quietly, changing tone.

I nodded.

"But you can't talk about it, huh?"

I shook my head.

Coney leaned back and sighed. "I knew something was up. You involved?"

"I am now," was all I said.

He didn't speak for a moment. If he wanted to ask me about it, he kept it to himself. He knew the rules.

"You know you gotta do what the Council wants you to, right?"

I nodded slowly.

Leaning forward, he spoke softly. "Don't do anything that'll jeopardize you or that great kid of yours. Do whatever the Council wants. Promise?"

My jaw dropped in shock. Did he know something? Was he warning me? Or did he just guess there was something serious on the line?

"I mean it, Gin. Promise me." His voice was sharp.

"Okay," I responded.

Coney leaned back and relaxed his shoulders. "You have a great thing going there. Romi's awesome. Take good care of her; because right now, she's the only one you can truly trust." With that, my cousin squeezed my hand and left.

Liv and the girls were asleep when I got back to the room. I climbed into bed. Coney wasn't entirely right. I trusted Liv and Dak. Maybe he'd been through some stuff with his family . . . maybe that's why he lived on the road. But my family was different. I always knew there were trust issues with other relatives. I mean, come on! With Richie for a brother and Lou for a grandfather, who wouldn't be a little paranoid?

I looked at the open door between my room and Liv's. Isn't it funny how in the dark your eyes see things in pixilated shadows? I trusted Dak. He'd never fail me. And Liv, well there was no question. If anyone could get me out of this mess, she could.

My mind wandered to my mother. I trusted her, but she was old school. Almost like Grandma—whom, by the way, I didn't trust. Then I thought about Romi. I smiled involuntarily at the way she'd acted at the induction. It startled me to think that someday she might see me like I see my own mother. No, she had to trust me. There could never be any doubt. I'd have to find a way to make her see that. She was already pissed off at what she saw as my betrayal at the ceremony. I didn't want her to grow up looking over her shoulder every five minutes.

And then Diego popped into my mind. He might think he trusted me, but when he found out I fed his client to a tiger, he'd probably change his mind.

Shit. I was already screwing everything up! I was starting to doubt the people I used to trust and had lost the trust of the two people I cared most about. If I got through this alive, I was seriously going to consider pursuing a career as a mystery novelist.

CHAPTER TWENTY-FIVE

*"You met me at a very strange time
in my life."*
—The Narrator, *Fight Club*

I used the free time on the flights home
the next day to think. I snagged one of
the legal pads from the resort (with the
family crest and motto on them and the
Bombay name as watermark) and started
scribbling notes on the private jet. Once
again, it was just Liv, me and the girls, so
we had some privacy.

I made up a page for each of the six
cousins, starting with Dak and ending
with Richie. Each page had a name, age,
address and basic statistics. What struck
me right away was that none of my male
cousins were married or had children. I'd
never thought about that before. That was
weird.

From there, I made a list of my modus
operandi. I would tap their phones and
search their homes. Liv would hack

into their bank accounts, credit card statements—all that stuff. I hoped this would give me enough information so I wouldn't have to come up with a reason to interview each of them.

Once I had the backgrounds all filled in—if I were lucky and the planets were in perfect, harmonious alignment, I could figure out their movements and compare them to the dates listed in the dossier of when the mole met with his confessors in D.C. and London.

Silently, I cursed the Council. I mean, it didn't make sense that they knew the dates Mole Man had had coffee with the feds, knew that it was a male from my age group, yet had no idea where to even start.

Okay, I'd get through it. I hoped I could at least cover this much territory in two weeks and give the Council what I knew. I had serious doubts I would have Mole Man in custody by then.

We sat in first-class from L.A. to Chicago. That gave me a little time to think, but not much. I eventually put my notebook away and picked up my knitting needles. I'd scored some bamboo yarn in L.A. and was eager to get started.

I was halfway through this cute, skinny scarf when we landed at O'Hare. Liv and I dragged two tired girls to our connecting flight, and within an hour and a half we were back home, trying to find our car in the airport parking lot.

When I dropped Liv and Alta at their house, we made plans to meet up the next afternoon. By the time I got home, wrestled Romi into the shower and bed and unpacked, I was too exhausted to pick up Poppy. Dad called and offered to keep her another day. And I slipped into a deep, dreamless sleep.

The alarm tore me from my sleep the next morning. I managed to get Romi dressed, fed and to school, making it back in time to jump through the shower before Diego arrived. As I skipped into my clothes on the way to the front door, I remembered that I'd forgotten to wash the sheets on my bed. Damn. And Diego wanted to use the bed this time. I briefly wondered if I could come up with some excuse before opening the door.

"Hey!" Diego pulled me against him for a mind-flattening kiss. My hair was still damp from the shower and I had no makeup on, but somehow, it didn't seem to matter. I pulled him inside and closed the door.

"Do that again." I sighed, flinging my arms around his neck. Diego laughed and kissed me again. He smelled like soap, which was now my new favorite smell. His skin was smooth from what I assumed was a recent shave. His breath was warm and tasted like peppermint. For a brief moment, I thought about flinging him over my shoulder and carrying him up to the bedroom like a cavewoman.

"I guess you missed me too," he said as he paused for a breath.

"Mmmmm, you have no idea." I kissed him again. I didn't want to talk about dead clients and I wasn't ready to find out about an upcoming trip to Australia. I would just have to distract him with sex.

We groped each other all the way upstairs to my bedroom. I panicked for a moment when I realized I hadn't washed the sheets or picked up the baskets of folded laundry (not that I ever did, really). But Diego's kisses were urgent and the warmth of his hands unfastening my bra pretty much took care of that.

I pulled off his shirt and pants and pretty soon the bed looked like we'd messed it up ourselves. In fact, I decided to tell him it was made originally.

Diego's touch turned my legs to jelly and my heart into a jackhammer. I craved every sound he made, every inch of his skin, especially when it met mine.

Obviously I was losing my mind, which is easy to do when a gorgeous man is licking your most sensitive parts. I decided to just go with the flow, before I exploded into a lovely, tingly orgasm. Then I climbed on top of that Australian body-guard and rode him until he came.

We didn't talk, just lay there tangled in the sheets. I was tired, spent and bliss-fully happy. It didn't matter what bad news Diego had for me. The sex was a Band-Aid. There was nothing he could say to make me feel bad.

"Damn. I'll miss you, Gin."

Except that! "What? When will you miss me? Why will you miss me?"

Diego leaned up on his arm and said, "My job is done here. Dead clients don't pay, or so the saying goes."

I sat up. "Do you have another job somewhere else?"

"Well, no. Not yet. But I doubt if I could find something here."

"Stay," I said. No, demanded.

"You're very important to me, Gin. There's nothing I'd like more than to set-tle down somewhere and have a home and family."

"So stay!" I tried not to sound pathetic, which was hard because I was naked in a messy room. "Here! With us!"

"I'd love to. But we really should talk about it first."

I was beginning to sound hysterical. "Why? What's there to talk about? Romi loves you! I . . ." I closed my mouth. Did I love Diego? How was that possible? No. I was just lonely and infatuated. That was all.

Diego politely ignored my outburst. "I'll stay for a little while so we can talk about this. I don't want it to go too fast. There's a lot we don't know about each other."

You have no idea. "Okay. That's a start."

"But I can't stay here. I'll check into a hotel."

"You can stay here!" I wanted to punch myself. How could I take care of this job and train Romi if Diego lived here? And what was I doing anyway? What kind of example was I setting for my daughter if I just let a strange foreigner move in?

"No." Diego reached for his pants. (Why was he reaching for his pants?) "It has to be a hotel. I don't want Romi to freak out. She's a great kid." He started to get dressed, so I did too.

"Okay, it's settled," I said, once we'd installed ourselves in the kitchen with coffee.

"It's far from settled," Diego began, "and honestly, I don't know what is going on in my head, but you've bewitched me. I can't even think of leaving."

Oooooh. That was so chauvinistic. Wasn't that always the way men put it? They didn't fall in love; the evil women cast spells over them.

"I hate that analogy," I muttered.

Diego looked surprised, and I realized it was the first time I'd ever seen him like that. "What? Oh. The bewitched thing? It's just a phrase."

Ohmygod! We were just about to have our first fight! "It also assumes that women are witches and men fall under their power." Way to go, feminist Gin!

He laughed. "I never thought about it that way. Sorry. I'll say it correctly then." He paused for what seemed like two years. "I'm falling for you. And I don't know what to do about it."

"Yaaaaayyyyyy!" I jumped up and down, punching my fists into the air. I kept up this action until I realized I wasn't actually doing it in my head, like I thought I was. Damn.

Diego laughed so hard that tears were rolling down his cheeks. "I've never gotten a reaction like that before!"

I forgot my embarrassment and folded my arms over my chest. "Do you tell many women that you're falling in love with them?"

He brought his hands up in protest. "No! That's not what I meant! You're the first since high school. But I love your reaction."

I grabbed his hands across the counter. "Diego, I think I'm in love with you too." I waited. "What? No little end-zone dance for me?"

Diego walked around to my side of the counter, lifting me onto it. I wrapped my arms and legs around him.

"Would you settle for a touchdown instead?" His voice was deep and I could feel him swelling between my thighs.

"Are we talking about football or soccer here?"

He closed his eyes and kissed me. "Football is soccer. And now I'm going to give you another lesson Down Under."

CHAPTER TWENTY-SIX

"We're going to have to redo every conversation we've ever had."
—John Smith, *Mr. & Mrs. Smith*

After some kitchen counter nookie and the promise to talk more that evening, Diego left to finish up some loose ends and check into a hotel. I should have felt guilty that I'd given him the reason for the loose ends, but I didn't. My demented mind told me that had I not knocked him off, Diego's client would be making plans to go back to his own hemisphere soon—taking Diego with him. Always look on the bright side!

I spent the afternoon installing my phone taps and setting my workshop for some serious chemistry. I'd decided to use a simple poison for the mole. It was colorless, odorless and instantaneous. Kind of like a sodium-pentathol shot for when you put down your pet. After all, Mole Man was family. And I at least owed

it to Richie, Lon or Phil to make it somewhat quick.

I'd ruled out Coney, Dak and Paris.
Coney may be odd and frightening to children, but I just didn't feel in my gut that
he'd turn in the family. No, it was definitely the creepy cousins.

The phone tap/iPod was set up in my lab
and plugged into my laptop. It would remotely cover all six phone lines, recording
the data on my computer. Okay, that was
done. Liv was going to need a few days to
get the financial information, so I went to
pick up Romi from school.

After plunking her in front of cartoons
with cookies and milk, I decided to wash
my sheets. Diego was coming by for dinner, and I wanted the bedroom to look a
little better than it had earlier.

I grinned, thinking of how the two of us
had managed to get all the sheets and
mattress pad off the bed without really
trying. It was a good thing my cousins
weren't surveilling me, because I bet I
looked pretty stupid standing in the laundry room with my face buried in the
sheets, trying to pick up Diego's scent.

Romi barely made it through dinner. She
was so tired from all the travel and a full
day of school that she actually excused
herself to go to bed. I tucked her in, then
joined Diego in the kitchen where he was

putting dishes in the dishwasher. My dishwasher! He looked like he lived here already. I tried to calm myself down. Slowly. *He wants to take it slowly, Gin.*

"You pay for dinner and clean up too? You're too good to be true!" I said, planting a kiss on his lips.

"Mum raised me that way. Can't really help it, I guess." Diego smiled.

"See?" I said, "You'd be a great asset around here. Not to mention a good role model for Romi."

"Hmmm." He laughed. "Are you pressuring me?"

"Absolutely. I want you here. What reason could you have for leaving?"

Diego frowned. "I don't want to leave, but there are reasons. I don't have a job, for one thing."

I wanted to scream, *But I'm rich! I have a huge trust fund! You'll never have to work again!* But I didn't.

"Money isn't an issue," was all I said.

"It is to me. Of course, maybe I could work with you. Or we could start our own company together."

I froze. I'd forgotten that he thought we were in the same line of work. While the feelings we had for each other were solid, I'd lied to Diego about my job and my family, and that was enough to screw everything up.

"Diego, I have to tell you something." I

looked him right in the eye to see how he
would handle it. "I'm not a bodyguard."
He arched his right eyebrow, and I completely chickened out. "Not . . . anymore,
that is. I haven't worked in a while." Lies
filled my head where the old lies used to
be, but I couldn't stop myself. "Ed left me
a lot of money. I don't have to work."

Diego smiled again. "I don't care about
that. I wouldn't care if you were an ax
murderer . . . that's not why I feel the way
I do."

I was pretty sure I flinched. No, I wasn't
technically an ax murderer. Well, there
had been that one time with a claw hammer, but I really didn't care for blades too
much. Of course, Diego had said he
wouldn't care if I were an ax murderer, so
maybe we had something to work with
here.

How would he handle the news I was an
assassin? If I got down on my knees and
confessed everything to him, would he
connect me to his client? And what if he
really liked his client? I was pretty sure
I'd be screwed.

"Whew!" I feigned wiping a sweaty brow.
"It's good to get that off my chest."

The kitchen was cleaned up, so we
grabbed a couple of bottles of beer and
went into the living room.

"Have you ever lost a client?" Diego
asked me.

"How are you holding up?" I dodged.

He took a long drink from the bottle, then turned toward me. "Reasonably, I suppose. It was quite a shock."

I put my hand on his thigh. "Tell me what happened."

Diego began with the day he had come by, looking for Vic Jr. He stepped out of the shower to find a note saying his client had taken a walk. Diego tried Turner's cell, but got no answer. He'd waited twenty minutes to see if his client would return. Then he drove around the neighborhood and thought of stopping by my house. After leaving me, he searched the neighborhood but came up with nothing. He spent the rest of the day calling work contacts, anyone connected to Turner. He ended with confirming his client's identity at the morgue.

"The zoo?" I lied, feigning shock.

Diego nodded. "I just had this weird feeling when I watched the news that morning. So I went to the police department and later identified the body.

I remembered that the body's head and neck had been mauled, "How did you identify him?"

"He had a Rolex with a personal engraving that was still on the body when they found him."

I didn't say anything for a moment or two. It had to be very, very hard to admit he'd lost a client. No matter what I said, it wouldn't make him feel any better.

For the first time in a long time, I felt remorseful for a death I'd caused. It wasn't like I was a psychopath or anything. I had a conscience. I just didn't usually feel bad about the lives I'd taken. They were all assholes, hurting innocent people for profit. But I never thought of them as having family, friends or colleagues who'd miss them after. I never really saw the impact my work had on other people's lives.

Granted, Diego wasn't a perfect bodyguard, or this wouldn't have happened. And I was merely a lucky assassin in that Turner had showed up unannounced . . . hell, practically gift-wrapped. But I'd done something that had hurt Diego, made him feel bad about himself. A reputation isn't a tangible thing, but when messed with, it can really screw you up.

"It's all right, Gin." Diego seemed to be reading my thoughts. "It was a freak thing. I can't protect my client if he sneaks off to do whatever it is he had to do."

"Does the company expect you to resolve the situation?" I had to know if Diego was going to hunt me down.

"No. Turns out he was laundering their money for terrorists. He never told me about his secret life. If he had, I would've resigned."

"Oh, come on. Aren't they all bad?" I joked.

Diego's smile faded just enough to let me know I'd screwed up. "I don't do the bad guys. I kind of have a thing about that."

Uh oh. "What do you mean?"

"I try to screen my clients. I'm not religious or anything, but I draw the line at those who have connections to killers, terrorists, that kind of thing."

A cold wash swept over me. People like me. "Not all killers are bad guys. What about soldiers, SWAT snipers, stuff like that?" Damn. The question popped out before I could think about it!

"Oh, I concede there are reasons to kill on a rare occasion. I just think of the others as nothing more than assassins. Killing for money. They're bad for business."

Nothing more than assassins? I knew what I did was wrong on many levels. But it was a time-honored tradition in our family. We kept things level. Maintained the balance for the circle of life and all that shit. Weeded out the wheat from the chaff. The scum from the good guys. Didn't we? Nothing more than assassins? He said it like it was a bad thing.

I couldn't focus. I'd go crazy trying to decipher things, but it appeared that my relationship with Diego could never work unless he warmed up to the idea that assassination wasn't necessarily bad.

"Come on, Gin," he swept a stray curl from my eyes, "I won't have a philosophical discussion on this."

He was right. "So what now?"

Diego relaxed, "I figured I'd give us a go. I'm not in any hurry to find another job."

I arched my eyebrow. "Give us a go?"

He responded by taking me into his arms and kissing me. After a few minutes, I came up deliriously for air.

"I've never felt this way before, Ginny. You're different from any woman I've ever known."

I nodded, pulling him by the arm toward the stairs. After all, I had clean sheets and everything this time. I checked to make sure Romi was dead asleep, before pushing him into my (newly cleaned) bedroom and locking the door.

Diego kissed me as he lowered me to the bed, "That's why I'm staying. At least for two weeks, that is."

Even though I was drowning in pleasure, this phrase hammered through my head: Why the hell did everything have to happen in two weeks?

CHAPTER TWENTY-SEVEN

"Contracts . . . neckties . . . high voltage! Done Dirt Cheap!"
—AC/DC, "Dirty Deeds Done Dirt Cheap"

I tried to put Diego's negative juju out of my mind when I woke up the next morning, alone, in my now not-so-clean bed. After dropping Romi off at school, I decided to put my head where it should have been all along and get with the assassination program.

I was delighted to discover that Missi's phone bug really worked. Lon, Phil, Coney, Dak, Paris and Richie had all made calls or answered the phone in the last twelve hours.

Unfortunately, none of the conversations had the words, "I'm talking to the FBI and the Yard." And one of Richie's calls was to a 1-900 number for transsexual dwarves (I'd need a lot of beer to scrape that from my brain—*shudder*), but I figured something would turn up.

I called Liv, but she was neck deep into some serious computer hacking, so I let her go with the promise we would get together for lunch the next day. That left the old standby—breaking and entering.

I guess it wasn't really breaking and entering when you already had a key to your brother's condo. But I didn't want the Council to think I'd slacked off on anything where my brother was concerned. Dak had called in the morning to tell me he was going to Chicago for an overnight with a blond something or other. Isn't that cute? As backup, we always let each other know when we were going to be out of town.

Anyway, I let myself in, waving at the old lady next door. She probably thought I was picking up his mail. She actually was a great neighbor for my brother. Completely deaf with an obsession for baking, Estelle took good care of him. I guess his charm was intergenerational.

I put the mail on the hall table and headed inside. Dak was surprisingly neat. He'd always been that way. Maybe to keep the bachelor pad looking good for the ladies. I walked through the apartment, checking for anything out of place.

Seriously, How did one go about looking for something incriminating on her brother? Especially when I didn't think he had anything to do with this mole thing. After a little floundering, I told myself to just search it like a regular hit, convincing myself that this would be excellent practice for when I searched my other cousins' places.

Carefully, I went through all the drawers in his room, pulling them all the way out to see if there were hidden panels or something taped to the bottom. Grandma would have been proud of me.

I tackled his closet, going through every pocket and shoe, looking for something I was convinced I wasn't going to find. The bed came next, as did the nightstand and the floorboards beneath the expensive Oriental rug.

I was relieved to have found nothing, which surprised me because I didn't expect to find anything. The bathroom and office were next. I went through each file meticulously. Nothing there but his diplomas, insurance, and health information. The living room and dining room were also clean. The sofa yielded only thirty-two cents and a stash of condoms.

All this clandestine searching made me hungry. No wonder! It was one-thirty. I found a Diet Coke and leftover pizza in the fridge. Hell, he wouldn't notice it was missing. I nuked two slices and opened his spice cupboard to find the garlic salt.

Odd. I rubbed my eyes and looked again. Dak hated Parmesan cheese. So why were there two large jars of it in the cupboard?

I snickered out loud. "Duh, Gin! Maybe it's for his guests." For some reason, I looked around. "Well," I said to absolutely no one, "I'm a guest."

I opened the first container and shook. It was very light, which normally would have told me it was empty, except for the weird rattling sound inside. Hmmm. Unless I was wrong, parmesan cheese rarely made a clunkety-clunk sound.

Maybe it had clumped up and hardened after sitting there for so long. I pried off the cap and looked inside. A small memory stick was all that was in there.

Okay. Lots of people backed up stuff. Family photos, important documents, that kind of thing. And hell, everyone in the family had secret hiding places, so it made sense Dak kept it hidden in the cheese can.

After convincing myself that was indeed the situation, I grabbed the other can from the shelf. After all, I still wanted Parmesan cheese. My heart sunk as I realized this can was also hiding something. A very thin cell phone popped out. It wasn't his standard phone, but hey, it was always good to have access to a wireless phone in an emergency. I replaced both items in their containers and sat down to eat the pizza.

The phone and memory stick stayed in the top right-hand corner of my head— like a weird computer icon. Even after I'd left Dak's house to pick up Romi, I couldn't get it out of my mind. And that was starting to piss me off.

Goddamned Council. They'd messed me up with this assignment. Believe me, there was nothing worse than an assassin who had lost her nerve. They'd turned me into a suspicious, nervous wreck! If anyone searched my house . . . and I mean really searched it . . . they'd find some weird shit too. It was just the way we Bombays operated. For two years, I had kept Romi's baby photos on microfiche hidden in a fireproof vault in the garden. Eventually, I'd come to my senses and stopped doing that, but it was a perfect example of how nuts my family was.

After picking up Romi, we collected Poppy from Dad. He seemed sad to let her go. But I missed her, and Romi needed her. We're not a normal family. So I reasoned we should do things that seemed normal. Like having a dog.

Diego came back for dinner again, this time bringing Italian carryout. Romi squealed with glee. Spaghetti was her favorite food. She'd eat it for every meal if given the chance. During dinner, I thought I saw Diego wink at her. Ahhhh. It worked. He'd achieved godlike status in her eyes.

I dropped the assassin subject from the night before because, well, because I didn't want to think about it. I loved everything about Diego. He was perfect! And we clicked. Same sense of humor, perfect chemistry in bed, and he loved Romi. He even read her a book at bedtime.

"She's a great kid," he said as he joined me in the kitchen a half hour later. Diego wrapped his arms around me from behind. He smelled wonderful. I leaned back and closed my eyes. I could really get used to this.

"Thanks. And nice job with dinner. How did you know it was her favorite?" I turned around and grinned.

Diego laughed. "Oh, she might have mentioned it at some point."

"So you're trying to win me by bribing my daughter?"

He shook his head. "I want to win her too. Remember, I love kids."

This time, we sat in the living room and talked for a couple of hours instead of going straight to my bed. We slipped into conversation comfortably. As we talked about hometowns and family, I realized how much I missed having someone to end the day with. With a start, I remembered that Ed and I had ended every night this way. Diego easily filled that role. The conversation steered to Romi and her school, and I was thrilled that he was so attentive. Apparently, Diego was just as interested in joining the family as I'd hoped he would be.

Of course, there was that rather sinister side of joining the family. But for now I focused only on the three of us.

"I'd love to take your family out to dinner some time."

"I'm sure Romi would love that."

He laughed. "No, I mean yes. You and Romi, but also your mum, dad and brother."

"Why?" I said before I could stop myself.

"Well, the circumstances I've met them under weren't exactly ideal. I'd like to get to know them. What do you think?"

Whoa. I guess he hadn't been kidding about the two weeks. Okay, why was this bothering me? He'd already met them. And I was pretty sure he would charm them to death. Hmmm. That might be worth exploring. I wondered if you really could charm someone to death. What a pleasant way to die.

I forced myself back on topic. "All right," I said, "How about tomorrow night?"

"Great! What's your mum's favorite place?"

I loved him hard right there. "Taschetta's. On Third and Twenty-second."

"What is it with your family and Italian food?" he teased.

"I don't know. We're Greek originally. Go figure."

Of course, the night ended in the bedroom. It's hard to describe how incredible Diego was in bed. Every time he touched me, I felt like the most desirable woman on earth. Our bodies moved together as if they'd been made to do just that one thing.

But while the sex was great, I found him even more mouthwatering because he loved my kid. He wanted to impress my mother. He wanted to meet my family. And he knew his way around a dishwasher. I wondered if I could wait for the two weeks to be over before I proposed.

As I watched him walk out to his car at three-thirty in the morning, I mentally wrote (in really girly handwriting) *Gin & Diego Bombay, 4-ever*. I bet I could get the Council to give me a year off after this assignment. Then I could take my time and tell my future husband everything. And we'd live happily ever after in a castle far, far away. Romi would be a princess, Diego would be the king, and I would be the queen of death.

CHAPTER TWENTY-EIGHT

"A desperate disease requires a dangerous remedy."

—Guy Fawlkes

Dak called in the morning, just as Romi and I were running out the door. He was staying a little longer in Chicago due to complications with a German stewardess. Could I take the mail in again?

In my typical mom-iform of yoga pants, T-shirt and jacket, I popped into his house and stacked the new copies of *Soldier of Fortune* and *Handgunner* and a plain brown package from Good Vibrations on top of the old mail. I was just about to leave when I remembered the cell phone and memory card. It occurred to me that the Council might frown on the fact that I hadn't checked them out, so I grabbed them and headed home.

I had a few hours until meeting Liv for lunch, so I hit the secret workshop and plugged the network card into my laptop.

"If I download a virus, Dak, you're so dead," I said to myself. My mind wandered a little, setting up different scenarios of how I would kill him if he messed up my laptop.

I breathed a huge sigh of relief when I saw that all the files were photos. I'm not sure what I was expecting—a list of undercover CIA operatives, the Dead Sea Scrolls, architectural plans for the Empire's Death Star? Photos I could deal with. Who knew the kid was so sentimental? I mean, he took millions of shots of my daughter every time he was around her. I clicked on the first file folder and opened it.

Here I was, thinking these were pictures of my precious little girl. So you can imagine how shocked I was to find a photographic record of my little brother's love life. Each folder was from a different conquest. And honestly? I had no idea there were so many uses for peanut butter and fishing line.

I didn't want to go any further, but I had to check them all out. I'd definitely have to use Lysol on my keyboard (and maybe my eyes) when I was done. And while I was impressed by how limber my brother really was, I didn't need to see these.

At last there was only one folder left. Then I could take a shower and don a hairshirt to punish myself. I clicked on the next file while squinting through one eye. But this file was different. There were no naked brunettes, acrobatic blondes or multi-orgasmic redheads. Had I hit the family pictures at last?

The first photo had Grandma in it. Only this wasn't your typical family album stuff. Grandma was kneeling over a man. A dead man, from the looks of the red blood splashed all over the room. In her left hand (I didn't know she was a lefty) was a .45 semiautomatic pistol.

I clicked on the next picture and saw a photo of Uncle Lou tossing a knife into the chest of a large blond man in a suit. This couldn't be right! Each photo depicted a family member making a hit. Why would he even have these? How could he have gotten them? Granted, we all wanted a little backup, but this was downright terrifying.

There it was, in full color—my family's profession. Every member was featured except for Dak, Mom, Paris, Liv and me. Was this some sort of insurance policy? I definitely needed to talk to my brother when he got home. This kind of shit was way too dangerous to have lying around . . . even if it was carefully hidden in a dried cheese can.

I tossed the memory stick into an envelope and stashed it in my safe. I hoped no one would ever find it there. I threw the cell phone in my pocket and headed to

Liv's for lunch. Maybe she'd have some kind of explanation for what I'd seen.

"Obviously," Liv rolled her eyes as she handed me a sandwich, "he gets turned on looking at pictures of his liaisons."

I made a face. "Not that! The other file. And by the way, why aren't you freaked out? You'd be totally grossed out if you found something like that at Paris's place!"

"Get over it. Your brother has sex with lots of women. Big deal." She took a bite of her tuna melt and chewed thoughtfully. I didn't even want to know what she was thinking.

"Okay, fine! Let's forget about those and focus on the"—I looked around and whispered—"family photos."

"I'd guess it's his insurance policy."

I shook my head. "I don't know. Maybe."

"Didn't you say you found a phone too?" Liv asked.

I nodded and pulled it out of my pocket.

"Oooh!" Liv cooed as I handed it to her. "I love these! I've been trying to get one, but there are waiting lists for this model."

I arched my right eyebrow. "Waiting lists? For a cell phone? What? Like for a Hermes Birkin bag?" I'd been on a wait list for that damned purse for two years! Who did I have to kill to get that bag?

Liv nodded, oblivious to my rant. "Yup."

She flipped it open. "These things are really rare. Top of the line too. I wonder why he'd hide it from us? Seems like Dak would want to show it off."

She had me there. My brother had always liked to flaunt his new toys. Why wouldn't he especially want Liv to know he had this phone, knowing her interest in all things technical?

"Hmmmm." She punched a few buttons. "That's weird. No numbers stored. I can't even find the number for this phone."

As if on cue, it rang. Liv and I froze, staring at each other. I didn't want to answer it, especially if it were some weird sex line he had. I shuddered, thinking there were women out there calling 1-900-DAKOTA. I really needed to talk to him. In spite of my mental meanderings, I did manage to jot down the number before it disappeared.

"Mind if I keep this a couple of days?" Liv asked. "Just for research, of course."

I nodded. "Any news on Dak's finances?"

Liv pulled her laptop over and logged on. "I went into Dak's and Paris's accounts, but didn't find anything unusual. Of course, if they had a Swiss bank account or something offshore, I wouldn't have it yet. I went ahead and checked on the others and there's no suspicious activity. You find anything?"

"No. Nothing." I rested my chin in my hand. This was very frustrating.

"So all we have is the memory stick and phone for Dak?" Liv asked. After I nodded she continued, "I'll see what my brother has at his place. He goes to the gym from ten a.m. to noon every day."

I loved Liv's brother as if he were my own. Paris and Dak were very close. They bragged about their bachelor lifestyles to me and Liv all the time. While my brother was fair, Paris had Liv's dark hair and eyes. Paris was not as much of a skirt-chaser as my brother, but he was very attractive and could really pour on the charm. He didn't have a specialty as far as the assassin thing went. Paris didn't like the idea of getting bored with too much repetition at work.

"Okay. Tell me what you find. I'll head home and see if I can get anything more on the phone tap. If not, I guess I'll be sending off the Chia Pets."

"I saw those in your suitcase," Liv replied, "but I thought maybe you ordered those from the home shopping network that night Richie saved your life. You were pretty drunk."

"Richie did *not* save my life!" Maybe I shouted that a little too loudly. I tried to look wounded as Liv erupted in giggle fits. "And those happen to be state-of-the-art listening devices from Missi!"

Liv wiped tears from her cheeks. "Fine. I'm sure the guys will love them."

CHAPTER TWENTY-NINE

"I guess it was just being in the wrong place at the right time. That's what assassination is all about."
—Andy Warhol

By the time Romi went to bed that night, I was in a full-blown panic. Dak wasn't answering his cell or home phone. I stopped by the condo with Romi after dinner, but there was no sign of him. Something was wrong. He always checked in. I even called Mom to see if she'd heard from him but only succeeded in worrying her. Fantastic.

The pictures of my family in the midst of "working" played through my mind like a twisted slide show. *And here we have Maryland in high productivity mode. Her output was exceptional in the last fiscal.*

There was no way I was going to sleep anytime soon. And Liv wouldn't have any news on Paris's place, nor would she have been able to run down any bank accounts in the Grand Caymans.

I found myself wandering into my lab. The light on the phone tap was blinking. I picked up my headphones and hit the replay key.

Coney had five messages from women in Truckee, all wanting to make "appointments." I had to smile. He had told me that in virtually every city there were wealthy, married women who wanted to sleep with him. There was something taboo about a one-night stand with a carny, he'd told me. I figured they picked him because he had all his own teeth.

"Master" Lon and "Master" Phil had a conversation with the NYC Order of Jedi Knights regarding an upcoming meeting of the Jedi Council in someone named Irving's basement. They were reminded to bring their action figures and not make too much noise so they wouldn't wake Irving's mom. There was also a message from, if I heard this correctly, female Klingon twins wondering if they were still on for their date to the Star Trek convention. Okay, so they weren't gay. But this was totally gross. It seemed to me that they were far too juvenile to be moles. And they'd need the trust funds to continue their Anakin Skywalker/Captain Kirk fetish. Ick.

I checked Paris's phone next. Nothing but a reminder from the dry cleaner. That left Richie and Dak. All my bets were on

Richie. I took a deep cleansing breath, and hoped I wouldn't hear another conversation with a gender- and height-challenged sex worker.

Nothing. Nada. Zip. The man hadn't even had a phone conversation in the last twenty-four hours. As I'd always suspected, he was socially retarded. What a surprise. Oh well. Something was bound to turn up. I checked Dak's phone.

After listening to a couple of messages from myself and a worried threat from Mom (my bad on that one), I actually got a recorded conversation.

"I don't know if I can do this." Dak's voice came through clearly.

"It's too late to back down now." A gruff, raspy voice sounding suspiciously like Eldamae Haskell (are the Girl Scouts involved?) replied.

"Do you have the stuff?" the voice growled.

There was a heavy sigh from Dak. "Yes. We're still on. I'll see you in D.C."

I sat in my chair for a long, long time. Forget panic—I was on the verge of full-blown hysteria. Dak couldn't be the mole! I looked at the memory card in my hand, the phone tap, and I would have looked at the cell phone if Liv hadn't confiscated it. No! There must be another explanation. But if so, why did everything I had in my possession say otherwise?

I examined the photos over and over—
but all I came up with was that Grandma
must have had highlights recently; killing
tall blond men gave Uncle Lou a boner
(my God, why did I have to see that?); and
that Lon and Phil liked to wear Yoda
masks when they did a job. Grandma's
highlights shocked me more than anything. Why try to look younger? It wasn't
like there was any age discrimination in
our profession.

I listened to the recorded phone conversation five times. I even tried calling his
home and cell phone again. But nothing
worked. The only thing left to do was go
to bed.

Of course, once in bed, I stared at the
ceiling. I squeezed my eyes shut and
willed myself to sleep, but it didn't work.
All I could see in my mind's eye was Dak
enjoying a mocha frappuccino with Bob
from the FBI and Nigel from the Yard.
*Here are the photos of my family killing
people, old chums. Could you please
pass the chocolate-pecan biscotti?* Finally, a few hours and three sleeping pills
later, I passed out.

I rang Liv's doorbell at eight-thirty a.m. after taking Romi to school. The door
opened, and Liv yanked me inside.

"I was just about to call you," she said,
sounding out of breath. Liv led me to the

kitchen and handed me a cup of coffee. My body was dragging after little sleep and an overdose of sleep agent. I needed the charge. Which was why I was surprised to taste rum in it.

"I found something," Liv said hurriedly, dismissing my arched eyebrow over the spiked coffee. "It looks bad, Gin. Have you heard from Dak?"

That was it. My heart unplugged itself from the arteries around it and fell into my feet.

"Did you check out the others?" I squeaked.

Liv nodded. "Your brother has an off-shore bank account."

"Swiss? Caymans?" I asked.

She shook her head. "Mongolia."

"Mongolia? There are banks in Mongolia?"

"Yeah. In Ulaanbaatar."

I stared at her. "Ulaanbaatar? Who hides money in Ulaanbaatar, Mongolia?"

Liv ignored me and continued. "Last month, someone from the D.C. area and from London deposited a total of five million dollars in Dak's account."

"That's got to be a lot of money for Ulaanbaatar," I replied.

"Will you give it up?" Liv shouted.

I gulped my drink and poured myself a mug full of rum, lightly laced with coffee. You ever have one of those days? Like when you find out your brother is working to put Grandma in jail and hoarding money in a bank in Mongolia? Well, I was having one of those days.

"Gin, none of the other guys has anything like this. Can you think of any reason he might have gotten so much money?" Her eyes pleaded with me, but I had no hope to give.

"Are you kidding? I can't figure out why he picked Mongolia!" Liv shot me a look that told me she would have me drawn and quartered if I mentioned it again. So I wisely dropped the whole Ulaanbaatar thing. Come on! Ulaanbaatar?

"That's not all," I started. I told her about the conversation I'd taped. "This looks really, really bad."

Liv shook her head, "No. I don't believe it. Dak wouldn't do this! He wouldn't sell us out."

I hated to be the voice of reason. I mean I *really* hated it. But I had to reply. "Liv, you, Paris, me and Mom weren't among his little 'Assassins Gone Wild' collection. He's not selling us out, just everyone else." At least there wasn't a photo of Grandma baring her wizened breasts and shouting "Woooooo!"

Her eyes grew wide. "Are you telling me you think your brother is Mole Man? Are you joking? Gin! This is Dak! He would never do this. Not in a million years!"

I looked at her with envy. I wished I could be so sure of his innocence. But doubt had installed itself firmly in my brain, and I couldn't ignore it.

"And what would be his motive?" Liv continued shouting, tears beginning to stream from her lovely eyes. "There isn't one! He adores living on the family trust fund! And he likes the job! There's no way you can convince me he is guilty!" She punctuated her rant by crossing her arms over her chest.

"Liv," I said wearily, running my fingers through my hair, "I don't know what to say. I don't want to believe it either. He's my baby brother, for Christ's sake! I baby-sat him! Taught him how to throw a football and zero the sights on a sniper rifle!" *Misty watercolor memories. Of the way we were . . .*

My cell phone went off, chiming AC/DC's "Dirty Deeds Done Dirt Cheap." It was the ring tone I'd selected for the Council back when I'd been optimistic about my life in the Bombay family. Of course, the deeds weren't done dirt cheap, but it seemed appropriate at the time.

"Hello?" I said warily.

"Gin. It's Dela. What do you have?"

"Nothing yet. I still have a week, right?"

Dela sighed. "We need to know as soon as possible, Gin. We can't wait until the last minute. Do you know anything?"

Sure. It's my kid brother. I'll deliver him hog-tied and bleeding tomorrow. Any particular appendages you want me to cut off and send you? "No. I'm still working on it. I'll get back to you as soon as I learn something." I clicked off the cell. Liv looked at me expectantly.

"It's the Council. We're running out of time," I told her.

Liv wiped her eyes on a dish towel and poured us both a glass of rum. We sat in silence for a moment.

"I haven't heard from Dak in two days. He's not answering his cell or home phone."

Liv's gaze drifted out the kitchen window. "I just find it so hard to believe. Are you sure you're not holding out?"

"Yeah. I'm protecting Richie. Jesus, Liv! How could you think that?" I shoved my rum aside. "What are we going to do?"

"We need to find him and confront him."

"Good idea. Of course, we can't find him, so that defeats the plan." Did I sound a little too sarcastic?

Liv threw her hands up in the air. "Well, I don't know! But we can't turn him in without talking to him about it first!"

"I don't even want to tell Mom. She would kill him. Of course, that would solve the problem."

"Okay. We need to take care of this right now." She picked up the phone and dialed. "Aunt Carolina? It's Liv. Gin's helping me with a job. Yes, it's in Chicago. Could you pick up the girls and Woody from school today? Thanks!"

I stared at her, my mouth open (which isn't really a good look for me). "How'd you get her to do that? I can't get her to do that!" Don't get me wrong—Mom loved the kids, but she was protective of her free time.

"I know. I figured she wouldn't be able to say no to me. So now that I've freed up the rest of the day, what should we do?"

CHAPTER THIRTY

"Martyrdom covers a multitude of sins."

—Mark Twain

Dak's condo looked exactly the same as it had when I left it. Liv figured that we needed to take a closer look at his place in an attempt to figure out what was going on. I hoped he'd come home and explain himself before I had to turn him in. So that's where we spent the afternoon— searching through my brother's things and getting drunk on the bottle of rum we brought from Liv's. We had given up the pretense of adding coffee hours ago.

"Maybe the Feds're using the photos of him with all those women as blackmail?" Liv slurred as she rummaged through his sock drawer.

"I dunno," I slurred back, trying to ignore the KY warming gel I found in his nightstand. "Why would he be afraid of those pictures? He's single. I can't think why they'd hold some sway over him."

"Oh my god! I've got it!" Liv rose to her feet so fast she lost her balance and fell onto the floor. I saw her hands appear on the top of the bed as she pulled herself up. "That's the reason you and I aren't on there! He's doing it to protect us!"

The room was starting to spin so much I had to lie down on the bed to keep from throwing up. "I don't gollow . . . fellow . . . follow."

Liv steadied herself against the headboard. "They approached him for evidence on the Bombays. They agreed to look the other way on us so Dak would do it!" Her crooked smile told me she was proud of herself for that theory.

I shook my head, making the room spin faster. "Whoa. The Council told me Mole Man approached the Feds. Not the other way 'round."

We lay on the bed for a while, trying to get the room to slow down and to wrap our liquefied brains around this idea. I think we even fell asleep because when I started moving around next, it was dark outside.

My skull felt like it was filled with cement and someone was trying to jackhammer through my forehead. I stumbled to the bathroom and found a spare toothbrush, then scrubbed for what seemed like an hour. I staggered back to bed and pulled the covers up over me and Liv, then turned over and fell asleep.

"I don't even know what to make of this," a man's voice rumbled.

Was I dreaming? It felt like it. My body had the sensation of being weightless and spinning counterclockwise.

"Gin? Liv?" the voice asked. I began to laugh.

"Shoot him!" Liv cried out in her sleep. This made me laugh even harder.

"What the hell is going on?" The man's voice was stronger now. And boy, did he sound pissed.

I opened my eyes slowly, willing my body to stop spinning. It did. I thought. Liv and I were snuggled up against each other, foreheads touching. The bedspread was pulled up to our chins, and we were fully dressed underneath. I tossed back the blanket and sat up. The digital alarm clock burned blazing red numbers into my brain. An empty bottle of rum lay on its side. And standing at the foot of the bed, with his arms folded, was my brother, Dak.

"Tractor!" I screamed at him.

Liv sat straight up. "What? Where?"

I pointed a finger at Dak. "There!"

She followed my finger with hooded eyes, which widened when they landed on Dak. "Tractor?"

I shook my head. "Yes! Traitor! That's what I said!"

Dak laughed. "You called me a tractor."

Liv and I scrambled to get to our feet, succeeding only in tangling our legs in the bedspread and falling, together, face first onto the floor.

"No, I said traitor," I declared once I had righted myself.

"What are you doing here?" Dak waved his arms across the room. "I get home to find you two drunk and in my bed, only to be called a tractor."

"I meant traitor." I glared at him as I tried to brush what felt like rhinoceros hair out of my teeth. "You're a regular Eggs Benedict!"

"Yeah!" Liv cried out. She had my back. Atta girl.

"So I've gone from being a farm implement to a breakfast food?"

"Huh?" He wasn't making any sense at all. But he wasn't gonna weasel out of this one. "Dak! You're the Mole Man!"

"Yeah!" Liv yelled, making my head hurt. "And you've been digging in the Bombay garden!"

I was getting confused, and Dak was as slippery as . . . well, something slippery. I stood straighter in a vain attempt to sober up.

"Dahhhkotahhh?" A female German voice trilled from the hallway.

"Ohmygod!" I screamed. "The Germans are in on this too?"

Liv assumed a defensive stance by raising her fists in front of her face. But something went wrong and instead she fell over, hitting her head on the footboard. She was out cold.

"Liv!" I shouted, climbing over the bed. Somehow I managed to snag my foot in the covers and ended up diving to the floor. At least, that's what I remembered before the world went dark.

I awoke in my bedroom without a clue as to how I got there. My body felt like shit, my head hurt, my tongue had been recently carpeted and there were some really strange bruises on my arms and legs. After hitting the ibuprofen pretty hard and gulping down two glasses of water, I took a shower and climbed into a pair of jeans and T-shirt.

Obviously, I wasn't dead. My brain thumped hard against my skull as if trying to get out. I didn't think I'd mind if it did. Romi wasn't in her room and it was ten a.m., according to the clock in the kitchen. After my third cup of coffee, the head pain began to subside and I noticed a note on the counter. It was from Dad. Apparently, Liv and I had made spectacles of ourselves at Dak's last night and so Dad had taken Liv home to her family and brought me here, while Mom kept Romi and took her to school this morning. Dad left one more note saying he was confiscating Poppy. Something about this being an unhealthy environment for a puppy.

Shit. The whole Dak betrayal flooded back and tears started coursing down my cheeks. How could he do this? I didn't even care what motivated him. It didn't really matter. My brother—my best friend—had sold his family down the river for . . . for what? Like I said earlier, it didn't even matter. I was pretty sure he didn't have an alibi that included anything like saving the lives of fluffy, homeless kittens or curing leprosy.

How ironic that I should be the one to turn him in. Maybe the Council had even known it was him and this was another goddamned test! I shuddered in spite of the warmth of my sunny kitchen. That idea hadn't occurred to me earlier. It would make sense (at least it would in my family) if the Council knew Dak was the traitor and sent me after him. Maybe they realized I was wary of training my daughter, or thought I'd lost my nerve.

That would seriously piss me off. I mean, I killed my lover's client—not only humiliating Diego, but putting him out of a job! Wasn't that enough? Now those octogeneric assholes were getting cheap thrills imagining me frog-marching my brother into the Brutus conference room at Santa Muerta.

My body started shaking. Too much anger and leftover alcohol was coursing through my veins. But if the Council had put me through this, I'd have to take them out. All of them. Even Grandma. Maybe especially Grandma.

Whoa, Gin! Is that what you're considering? Killing off the leaders of the Bombay Family? That's just crazy talk! My schizophrenic side kicked in, responding appropriately. *Is it?* Wouldn't it be worth it to be rid of this family curse, once and for all? I was pretty sure my cousins would be happy with it. Our trust funds exceeded 100 million dollars . . . each. We'd all live pretty comfortably for the rest of our days.

My hands shook as I held my coffee cup. Why hadn't anyone thought of this sooner? I mean, wasn't Grandma pissed when her brother took out her daughter all those years ago? Wasn't it reasonable to assume that someone, somewhere down the line had tried at some point to put their foot down?

Maybe we were all genetically deprived of rebellious thoughts. Could be the family had found a way to remove whatever DNA strain exists that would make us question authority.

I set the coffee mug down. I had to. My hands had lost control, and I wasn't fond of third-degree burns. I forced myself to sit. All of these thoughts swirled around in my head, making me nauseated. Or was that the hangover? Standing up, I went to the fridge and got out some bacon to fry. Greasy food always helped me think.

By my second plate of bacon, I started to relax. By the third, I felt better. Rational thought was what I needed. Bear in mind, I consumed half a pound of bacon in order to realize this. I revisited the conspiracy theories. It hurt to think that my family could knowingly cause me so much pain. Diabolical as they were, I still loved them. Well, all but Richie. I couldn't even *like* that bastard.

Was it really possible that I'd been set up to do this shit job? It sucked that I couldn't tell anyone, because I could use some advice from Mom or Dak.

Dak. Dakota Bombay. He was questioning authority, wasn't he? He'd found a way to rebel. And his carefree attitude showed he could still sleep at night. But why?

I shook my head. This wasn't getting me anywhere. "Dirty Deeds" chimed from my cell phone. It was the Council, or at least Dela. How long could I stall her? I answered it—mainly because a small part of me wondered if they had implanted an explosive device in my brain and could set it off at will.

"Gin." Dela's usually calm voice sounded frantic. "What do you know?"

"Nothing more than yesterday." Okay, so I lied. Sue me.

She sighed into the phone. "We're running out of time, Gin. The Council thought you'd come through before now."

Was that a threat? Or was my conspiracy-addled brain thinking it was a threat? If a family conspiracy happens, but all of the Bombays are dead, is it really a family conspiracy?

"I'm using some high-speed stuff Missi gave me," I stalled. "I should have something for you in a couple of days."

"I don't know if we can wait that long," Dela replied.

"What do you mean?" I shouted. "You guys gave me two weeks! Why did you give me two weeks if you really wanted it in one?" Okay, cross me off for an appointment in the diplomatic corps, but I was pissed.

"I know we said two, Gin. But what we meant was immediately. The Council's afraid the mole will bump things up."

I adopted a very juvenile posture (good thing she couldn't see me). "Oh yeah? Well, how do I know that *you* don't know who this guy is?"

There was a pause in the conversation and I thought that wasn't good.

"Do you really think we'd set you up?" Dela was not exactly happy. "If we knew, we would've made a very public example of him at the reunion. Do you think we're idiots, Gin?"

Time for some damage control. "I'm sorry. My mind's just running wild over this whole thing."

"I understand, Gin, but the fate of the Bombays rests on you. Find him!" Dela hung up.

I clicked off the phone, thinking I'd made it to the most miserable point in my life. My attitude hadn't helped. Oh well. Screw 'em. As long as they couldn't tell I was stalling, I didn't care what they thought. At least it would be another twenty-four hours before I heard from them again.

So, what did I know? I felt pretty sure they didn't know Dak was the one. There had been only one time in our history— about three hundred years ago, I think, when an example had been made at a family reunion. I seem to recall it included thumbscrews, feral weasels and strategically placed raw meat. Ugh.

Okay, I had time on my side. And they didn't know who the mole was. Maybe if I got Dak to convince them this was one big misunderstanding . . . But how could I

do that? It wasn't like he had accidentally
made appointments with agents from
D.C. and London, then accidentally kept
the appointments and accidentally promised them information, then accidentally
followed every Bombay until they made
hits and accidentally recorded the hits on
a digital camera. No, I'd say they wouldn't
buy that.

I had to talk to Dak immediately. I
needed to know why he did it. Maybe
there was some miniscule, remote chance
I could save him. I had started to reach for
the phone when I heard the doorbell.
Checking the monitors, I saw it was
Diego. Wow. Did he have bad timing or
what?

CHAPTER THIRTY-ONE

"Ita feri ut se mori sentiat."
("Strike him so that he can feel he is dying.")

—**Suetonius**

"Hey, Gin," Diego started, then stepped back, scrutinizing me. "Are you all right?"

Damn. I'd been crying earlier. I must've looked like a depressed Hamburgler. Maybe I shouldn't have answered the door.

Diego stepped inside, a worried look on his gorgeous face. I closed the door, then dove into his arms. It felt so good to be held. The tears came and I gave up all shreds of dignity as I sobbed against him. My life felt like it was coming apart at the seams. But now I had someone whose shoulder I could cry on. Horrified by my obsessive use of clichés, I squeezed Diego tighter.

"Shhh," he whispered, "it's all right. Everything will be okay." His hands slid up and down the length of my back, and each stroke felt like a release. It had been too long since a man had comforted me. Diego took to it like he'd been born to support me. Most men would have behaved awkwardly, as if not sure they were doing the right thing. But somehow I knew Diego was genuinely concerned and wanted to help me. He never asked me what was wrong—he just knew he could help.

My sobbing slowed, but my tears came faster. That simple act of holding me had more meaning than anything else he could've done. This man cared about me. And I knew right there and then that I was in love with Diego Jones. The longer he caressed and cooed, the more fiercely I loved him. Like the Grinch, my heart felt like it grew three sizes in that one moment.

I squeezed my eyes closed. This was a defining moment in my life. I had just learned that I was in love with this man and would do anything to make him happy. Dak may have broken my heart, but Diego was healing it without a word. How cool was that?

Dak. He was the reason I was so upset—and hungover. My darling brother had betrayed us all. And I had to punish him. But how could I? My arms gripped Diego's body as I realized that there was no way I could hurt Dak.

An idea started to grow. Maybe Diego could help me. Maybe I didn't have to deal with this alone. Hope bubbled in my blood. It had been a long time since I'd had help. I missed having a partner in my life. And Diego had potential to be the partner I never had with Ed. My chest inflated with hope. This was what I needed.

Diego continued soothing me until I choked off my last sob and pulled away.

"Thanks, Diego. You don't know how much that meant to me." I wiped my eyes with the back of my hands, leaving black, inky trails on them.

"Would you like some tea?" I managed to squeak out. He nodded and followed me into the kitchen.

I knew I looked like hell. In the movies, women look beautiful when they cry. But the truth was clear to me when I saw my reflection in the kettle. Red, puffy eyes ringed with smeared black mascara. Teenage Goth girls had nothing on me. I excused myself for a moment and raced to the bathroom to clean up my face.

"Diego, I'm so sorry . . ." I began when I returned.

He held up his hands to stop me. "It's not necessary. I figured something was up when you and your family didn't show last night."

Last night? What the hell was he . . . oh no! I was supposed to invite my family to dinner with Diego last night! With everything else, I'd completely forgotten! I'd completely blown him off. In fact, he was probably over here to make sure I was alive. I didn't think it was possible to feel so terrible.

So I did the mature thing. I started crying. The tea kettle whistled and there I was, weeping like an idiot.

Diego started toward me but I stopped him.

"I really screwed up. I forgot all about the dinner. I didn't even ask my family. That's the problem."

Diego just nodded and I realized I wasn't really making any sense.

"It's my brother . . . Dak. He's . . . he's . . ." I couldn't finish. What was I going to say? *Dak betrayed the whole Bombay family, turning us in to the FBI and Scotland Yard. And he's too old to spank. In fact, the Family wants me to kill him. How are you with an ice pick?*

I looked at Diego. He smiled patiently. He wasn't going to pressure me into telling him before I was ready. And I loved him even more for that. I was just getting to the part where I was mentally designing the wedding invitations when he spoke up.

"Is there something I can do?" He was sincere. Something in those simple words told me he would do all within his power to make the hurt go away. I had to trust him. I wanted to trust him. It was a low moment of complete insanity, but hey, I had nowhere to go but up.

"Diego, there's something I have to tell you. I hope you don't have anyplace to be for a while." I sat down and pushed his cup of tea toward him.

Diego leaned back and relaxed, a smile on his face. "Gin, you can tell me anything. I want to help. I don't have to be anywhere but here." He reached across the table and took my hand in his. "I love you, Gin. I want you to know that before you tell me whatever it is."

My body melted into a little puddle. "I love you too, Diego!" I would've shouted it from the floor, had I really melted.

Unfortunately, I didn't have time to celebrate. "That means so much to me. What I have to tell you isn't going to be easy to hear. In fact, I'm forbidden to tell you at all." I took a deep breath. "But here goes."

I paused dramatically before continuing. "Diego, I never was a bodyguard. It's quite the opposite, really. I'm actually an assassin." I waited for the words to sink in, which, by the way his face fell into shock, happened sooner than I thought.

"You're an assassin? Is this a joke?" Diego frowned.

"No." And so I began to tell him everything. About my family, our history and mission in life (and, I guess, in death).

And let me tell you, the Icelandic Sagas weren't this long. I would also hazard a guess that they weren't this interesting either, judging by the way his mouth hung open. Then I launched into the family reunion and the quest for the mole. I finished with the evidence that pointed to Dak. The whole thing took two hours and would have been a lot easier to deliver with a snappy multimedia presentation, but I only had so much to work with, and time was running out.

Diego sat there silently for a while, absorbing every word I said. I could tell at the beginning that he thought I was kidding. That made sense, though. Who would believe it? It's a pretty weird story.

"Do you have anything stronger than tea?" Diego finally asked. I nodded and pulled a bottle of wine out of the cupboard, opened it and poured it into two glasses. The first sip gave me a high, stemming some of my hangover. I usually didn't drink on a hangover. But then I usually didn't get drunk either. At this point, I really had to say that scruples were for suckers.

I watched impatiently as Diego drained his glass. This wasn't something I could rush, even though it would've been nice if he'd said, *That's great! I'll take on the Bombay name! Let's get married and I'll help you with your work!*

Instead, he looked me right in the eye. "So you're an assassin. And your whole family—your mum, your brother—are all assassins. And you have to turn Romi into one?"

I tried to read into his words as I nodded. "I know it sounds crazy." I shrugged. "I just grew up with it. I haven't really known it any other way." Okay, I fibbed here. I knew it was wrong. But I needed some sympathy.

He sat back, filling his glass again. "Did you ever realize that it's wrong to kill people?"

Whoa. I didn't expect that. "Yes, I know it's wrong to most people. But everyone I take out is really bad. Terrorists, spies, murderers . . ."

"People like you," Diego said quietly.

"Um, I don't, well, yeah. Sort of." I was confused. "I mean, I'm not a terrorist or spy."

"But you are a murderer, and have been since you were fifteen. Right?" Diego's voice was very, very calm. Like, eye-of-the-hurricane-in-the-Bermuda-Triangle-on-Friday-the-Thirteenth-with-a-black-cat-and-ladder-in-your-boat calm.

My stomach flip-flopped. "I usually have only one job a year. This month was unusual in that I had two, but they were both bad guys. One was selling military secrets to the Chinese and the other used corporate money to support South American terrorists."

Diego buried his face in his hands and I realized this was going to be a lot harder than I thought. All of a sudden, I started to panic. What had I done? I'd never even told Ed any of this! Aaaaahhhhrrrg! The jackhammer left my head and started on my heart. I was pretty sure that after this next glass of wine, it would go after my liver.

"Gin, I'm trying to wrap my mind around this." Diego struggled and I knew it was the truth. "I want to believe there aren't really people like you out there."

"We just take care of people the government can't. The U.S. doesn't sanction assassination. We . . ."

"So you're a patriot?" he asked doubtfully.

"I don't know about that," I answered.

"So you just do it for the money?" he countered.

I shook my head. "I'm not a profiteer! I'm not a mercenary! But I don't necessarily do it for my country." It hit me. I had never really questioned what I did. Why was that?

"Dammit, Gin!" Diego stood and shoved the chair away. "I don't know what to say! I want to buy in, but it's against everything I ever believed!"

"I can understand that. It's never easy

to tell someone outside the family. I know it's difficult to accept. And it was unfair of me to unload this on you." The wine left a dry, tangy feeling in my mouth. I grabbed a bottle of water from the fridge and drank.

"Do outsiders usually have problems dealing with this?" Diego asked.

"Yes. I guess. I don't know. I never told Ed." A small part of me felt like I was betraying his memory by telling Diego. How could I tell him when I never told my husband?

His eyebrows arched in surprise. "You never told Ed? Why?"

I sat down. Why hadn't I told him? "I guess I didn't think he'd take it very well."

"I can understand that," Diego said quietly.

"So, I blew it with you, huh?"

"No, Gin. You didn't blow it with me. I still want you. But I have to come to some kind of understanding with this. And I'm pretty sure I don't want you to do it anymore."

"You have no idea how much I agree with you." I licked my lips. "It's not like it's easy. Granted, I've fostered a pretty cavalier attitude toward it my whole life. But it's not an easy lifestyle to accept." Dak was the main example of this.

"Well, first I guess we should deal with

your problem. Then maybe we can take a long vacation and sort this out."

My heart exploded! Diego was going to help me! And then there would be a vacation! Maybe with lots of sex! I ran over and climbed into Diego's lap, kissing him frantically.

"I love you so much!" I said between kisses. "I never thought I'd find someone like you. Not in a million years!"

Diego pulled back. "Hold on there, Gin. Air must flow to my brain in order for me to think."

I leaped off his lap and returned to my seat. "Right. Solution first, sex later."

Diego laughed and I felt wonderful. Surely nothing could ever screw this up!

"You said you had two jobs this month? Anyone I know?" I was pretty sure he was joking.

I could feel my skin burning. Why did I say that? I was going to tell him, someday, about his client. Now was not that time.

So I lied to the love of my life. "No. No one you know."

Diego's eyes narrowed. My heart bounced around in my chest. Surely he couldn't see my treachery. Damn. My hands were shaking.

I watched as his eyes grew wide with realization. "No! No! It can't be!"

Diego was too smart to fall for my bullshit. My only hope was that maybe he could handle it.

"Diego, I . . ."

"You killed my client?" His shock was pretty clear. "You murdered Turner?"

I stood up. "I had to! It's not like we have a choice!" I was an idiot to think he would still love me after hearing the truth.

"You put me out of work! You set this up from the beginning! Oh my god!" He started pacing, running his hands through his hair. "You stalked me at the bookstore, lured me to your table. You seduced me in order to get Turner!"

What? "What? No! I didn't know when I met you that I'd be assigned your client. It was just a weird coincidence. That's all!"

Diego shook his head. "I can't believe I was so stupid! Not only am I a failure at my job, I'm an idiot too!"

Uh oh. This was very, very bad. "No, you're not. You had no idea who I was. I didn't get the assignment until after our first date. I didn't trick you!"

Diego's eyes betrayed his pain. "How could I be so stupid? I fell for you hook, line and sinker. I played right into your hands."

"Now wait a minute. If I were really conning you, I wouldn't have told you all this."

"Turner was my client. You had to know that before you took him out." He wasn't shouting, but he might as well have.

"Honestly, Diego! I didn't know he was your client until after I killed him—when you came looking for him that morning!" Oops. What was wrong with me? Can't I keep my mouth shut for two minutes?

He turned a scary shade of pale. "I didn't really believe it until you just now said it. You killed Turner. You lied to me when I came over. Why, he was probably on his way to the zoo at that very minute!"

I was mad now. "Well, that shows what you know! He was dead on my living room floor while I talked to you at the door." I clapped both hands over my mouth, as if that would take back the words I shouldn't have said.

"You're nothing more than a murderer! A common killer!" Diego exploded. "I'll bet you thought it was real funny—humiliating me like that."

"Hypocrite! You had no idea who Turner was! You told me you don't work for the bad guys. Ha! You didn't even know he was funding terrorist activities south of the border. He was evil, and I did my job!"

Diego sneered. "Yeah. You were just doing your job. That of a hired killer. Some career path!"

"Oh yeah? Well, at least I did my job

well! My client didn't die at the hand of my girlfriend!"

Everything suddenly went into slow motion, like we were walking through water. I knew I had screwed up royalty before the last word left my mouth. I had taken Diego's humiliation and shoved it up his ass.

"Good-bye, Gin," Diego said very quietly. He turned toward the door.

"Diego, wait! I'm sorry!" I ran after him, but he pushed me aside.

"It's too late for that. Don't worry, I'll keep your secret. But I never want to see you again." And then, Diego Jones walked out of my door and out of my life.

CHAPTER THIRTY-TWO

"That's the key to our team. We have so many weapons. You can just pick your poison."

—Steve Nash

So this was what it felt like to lose everything. Well, almost everything. I still had Romi, but from the looks of things, she was headed for the same trouble I was in, in about thirty years. Diego was and soon Dak would be out of my life forever. And it was all my fault.

Okay, so maybe I had nothing to do with Dak being the mole, but I would be responsible for his death. Can you even imagine what it was like to go from absolute elation to complete despair? Diego had told me he loved me. He was even starting to accept me, and I had to mess it up beyond all recognition.

It was as if I'd forgotten how to breathe. Or maybe I didn't want to anymore. In fact, if it weren't for Romi, I would have taken myself out right then. The pain was crushing—like being on the canyon floor when Road Runner drops an anvil-shaped boulder on you. Or at least, that was how I saw it.

I'd had love in the palm of my hand. And I'd willingly thrown it away. No. That was too soft. I'd given it a thousand paper cuts and pushed it into a lemon juice bath.

I probably would've spent several days lying on the floor by the front door, wallowing in self-pity. That is, if Liv hadn't found me a couple of hours later.

"What the hell are you doing?" she cried.

"Oh, nothing. Just dying. Make sure I get cremated. And I want you to have that Hello Kitty lamp in my workshop." The hard floor had numbed all feeling in my extremities, but I just stayed there, punishing myself. It kind of made sense, really. I'd caused Diego all kinds of pain. He thought I had conned him so I could get closer to his client and kill him. Diego believed I'd never loved him and knew I murdered Turner. He must have felt horrible. First he'd failed at his job; then he'd lost his heart to a heartless assassin who used him.

That wasn't the case, but he believed it. In Diego's mind, I had hurt him in every way possible. And I hated myself for it.

"Are you going to get up and tell me what happened or do I have to lie down there too?" Liv looked down at me.

"You could speed things up by putting a bullet in my brain. Or I have a lovely colorless, odorless, fast-acting poison that tastes like Godiva chocolate," I responded.

"What happened, Gin?" Liv sat next to me, legs crossed. I told her everything. Why not? Soon I'd kill my own brother, and then I'd have to raise my little girl to follow in my evil footsteps. I couldn't hate myself any more than I already did.

"Wow. You're evil," Liv replied. She threw in a whistle for emphasis. "Poor Diego. I can't imagine what hell he's going through."

I nodded in agreement, even though it hurt my head to do so.

"So, aren't you going to go after him?"

I shook my head. "I can't. He's right. I'm such a death-dealing bitch. Diego deserves better than me." I switched to an Australian accent. "Maybe he'll move back to Australia. Marry a sheila and settle down to raise a bunch of bruces."

Liv grabbed me by the arm and pulled me up. "You are so pathetic."

I pulled my arm away. "Easy for you to say. You're happily married to a wonderful man and you didn't have to kill his boss. And let's not forget you don't have to hunt down your own brother."

Liv responded by dragging me to the kitchen and making me a cup of coffee. Then she called Mom and asked her to

pick up the kids from school. I sat and
listened while she got Todd to pick up
their kids and then called Dak, asking
him to come over. I said nothing throughout. I just sat there, drinking coffee and
picking at all my emotional scabs over
and over again.

Liv sat down. "Dak's on his way. I think
we should focus on this problem first.
Then you can talk to Diego and explain
things. You fell pretty hard for him,
didn't you?"

I nodded. "He told me he loved me. So,
I told him I killed his client and ruined
his life. Pretty much par for the course
for me."

"Well, channel that frustration into
something useful." She nodded in the direction of the doorway as Dak came into
the kitchen.

She was right. I'd saved up a lot of anger
and now I had a place to spend it. For now,
I needed to focus. Diego was still alive.
But Dak might not be for much longer.
One thing at a time.

My older sister mode kicked in. "Sit," I
told Dak, pointing to a chair. He looked at
me with a mix of confusion and fear.
Good. *Feel my wrath.*

"What is your problem? Liv and I know
what you're doing. Now we have to find a
solution so I don't have to kill you," I said
levelly.

"Gin, what the hell are you talking about?" Dak asked, his eyes wide open.

"You're talking to the FBI and Scotland Yard. You're getting ready to turn the Bombay Family in! And I've been assigned to kill you." I was now channeling Dirty Harry. I tried to do that little Clint Eastwood squinty thing. I could go upstairs and get my .44 magnum, but the pause would detract from my dramatic approach.

Dak looked from me to Liv, eyes widened even further in shock. "What? There's a mole in the family?"

Liv crossed her arms over her chest. "Don't play games with us, Dak. You have some serious explaining to do."

"I don't know what you're talking about! I'm no traitor." Recognition sprang into his expression. "Hey! You called me a tractor last night! Is this what that was all about? Helga was pretty freaked out."

I nodded.

Dak rose from his chair. "I didn't do it! Why would I try to take down the family?"

Liv chewed her lip, looking at me. I could see her faith was faltering.

"Wait here!" I raced to my workshop, grabbed the memory stick and laptop. I hoped Liv had brought the cell phone. I joined them in the kitchen.

"Look what I found at your house!" I plugged in the stick and ran the photos.

Liv cocked her head to the side, eyebrows arched at the pictures of Dak's conquests. When it got to the family photos, Dak just stared.

"And how do you explain the cell phone?" I demanded. As if on cue, Liv handed Dak the phone. He looked at it as though it might sprout teeth and bite him.

"I . . . I don't know what to say." Dak had gone pale. I had him.

"Why, Dak? Why did you do it?" Liv pleaded.

He turned toward her. "I didn't do anything! That's what I'm trying to tell you! I never took those pictures! I don't know how the hell anyone got a camera in my bedroom." Dak pressed a button and went back through the photos. "Or the kitchen and the living room . . . and the garage. And I don't know anything about this!" He held up the phone. "Really, Liv! If I had one of these—I would have shown it to you!"

Liv and I looked at each other. I guess we had just expected him to admit he did it. It hadn't occurred to us that he'd deny it all.

I rubbed my forehead. "Dak. Just admit it so we can figure out how to save you."

His face turned red. "But I didn't do it! Why don't you believe me?"

Liv said, "It's too late for that. Don't deny it. That's just wasting time. The Council's been calling Gin every day— harassing her into producing the mole."

"We have to deal with this, Dak. There's no time to pretend it's not you. Let's just move on."

"I didn't do it!" Dak protested. "I swear, I've never seen this shit before."

"So I suppose you've been framed. Is that it?" I said rather sarcastically.

"Yes! That must be the answer!" Dak nodded furiously. "Someone is setting me up. Probably the guy who really did this."

I sighed, feeling the weight of the situation settle into my bones. Dak was sticking to his story. Liv and I were frustrated. We either had to tie him to a chair and get a confession out of him, or I had to render him unconscious and deliver him to Dela. Either way, we were going to be here a while. I sighed again and picked up the phone to order pizza. *What?* I never had lunch! Remember? I was lying on the floor for hours.

I hung up the phone after ordering. No specials today. Dammit. "Okay, we have thirty minutes to work this out. Then we eat. After that, we stay here until we have a plan. Okay?"

By the time the pizza arrived, Dak was still maintaining his innocence. Liv and I were exhausted from pleading and threatening him. So we spent twenty minutes in silence, eating pizza and drinking beer. I looked at the clock. Was it really evening already? Finally, I went to my studio and

grabbed my iPod phone tap device, wondering why I hadn't thought of it earlier. I
brought it into the kitchen, attached
speakers and plugged it in.

"All right," I began, "how about this?" I
played Dak's conversation. Twice.

Dak slapped his hand against the table.
"That's not me!"

I rolled my eyes. "For Christ's sake,
Dakota! It's your voice on your phone!
Who the hell else would it be?"

Liv leveled her eyes at him. "You have
to admit, we've got you on this one."

Dak buried his face in his hands, reminding me of Diego's similar action that
same morning. I brushed the thought
from my mind.

"I swear, Gin," he said slowly, "I wasn't
home when that call was made! I am not
the mole! I know it looks really bad, but I
didn't do it!"

Something in the way his voice cracked
on the last word caught me off guard. It
opened the door slightly and a little bit of
doubt slipped in. I rubbed my temples. Either I was terrible at getting a confession
(I'm not really trained for that), or Dak
was telling the truth and I was wasting
precious time. If I hadn't driven Diego
away, maybe he would know what to do. A
piercing pain shot through me and I re-
jected thinking about Diego again. At
least for the time being.

I looked at Dak. Did I really not trust him? Was he telling the truth? I was completely clueless and, after glancing at Liv, realized that she was too.

"I don't know what to do," I confessed. As if saying it out loud would make an answer miraculously appear. In that moment, I longed for the days when all I'd had to worry about was Vivian Marcy and my little Daisy Scout troop.

Dak reached across the table and took our hands in his. "I swear that I am innocent." The exhaustion and worry in his eyes convinced me. He wasn't the mole.

The phone rang; caller ID said it was Mom. I sighed again, realizing she wanted to know when I'd pick up Romi.

"Hey, Mom," I answered.

"Gin! Thank God! I tried your cell, but it wasn't working. I tried Dak and Liv, but couldn't get them either." Had Mom been hitting the coffee a little too hard? She said this so fast I could barely keep up.

"Sorry. I'll be by to pick up Romi in an hour or so."

"No!" she shouted. "You can't! She's not here!"

And just when I thought I couldn't panic any more. "What? Where is she?"

"The Council took her! Gin! What are you involved in? Lou said you weren't cooperating, so they were taking her to Santa Muerta until you did!"

I sat down on the floor. Dak and Liv
looked at each other. Dak, hearing Mom
screaming from the phone, pried it from
my grip and talked to her.

All I heard was "blah, blah, blah." Romi!
My little Romi. First Diego, then Dak, now
Romi! What had I done to deserve this?
The Council had gone too far this time.

I stood up, grabbed my cell and called
the Council's hotline. And yes, their phone
was red.

"Hello, Gin," Troy answered in his
snooty accent. "You must have received
our message."

"Troy, you limey peasant-fucker!" *Limey
Peasant-fucker?* "What have you done
with her?" I screamed.

"Gin, calm down. We won't hurt her as
long as you turn over the mole."

"You touch her, and you die!" I shouted.
And I meant it. This time the Council had
gone too far. Maybe it was time I ended
the Bombay Family business—once and
for all. "I'll see you real soon." I hung up.

Dak's face was twisted with worry.
"Mom says they're taking her to Santa
Muerta. I told her not to come over. She
wants to go with us, but I think we should
handle it."

"My God, Gin! I can't believe they took
her!" Liv whispered, hugging herself. I
could see in her eyes that she was afraid
this might happen to her someday.

"Well." I pulled myself up to my full height. It was time to channel the cowboy Clint Eastwood. "We're going to Santa Muerta. We're getting Romi back. And then I'm gonna kill each and every one of them."

"I'm in. But what about the mole?" Dak asked.

"Screw the mole! Hey! Let's bag Richie and deliver him!" I was losing it, laughing maniacally.

"Gin?" Liv said. "The light is blinking on your thingy." She pointed at the faux iPod. I thought of flinging it against the wall, but something deep inside told me to give Missi's invention one more chance.

I pushed the button and we listened. It was Richie's line. And he was in mid conversation.

"It was so easy. That bitch Gin is so stupid. She didn't even know I was following her." My mind rewound to that night in Vic's house when I had seen a man in the den. "It was so easy to tell Turner she was an assassin and convince him to go to her house." I thought about Diego. "But setting up Dak was the best idea I've had yet!"

Liv pushed the save button and stopped it. "We need this, Gin. To play for the Council." She was right in thinking I was about to destroy the damned thing.

"It was Richie?" I squeaked. "How could I be so stupid?" *How did I get so lucky?*

"Dak, delete the photos of you from the memory card but keep the family pictures. In fact, download them onto my laptop. Liv, you don't have to go with us. You have your own family to think about."

Liv shook her head violently as Dak plugged the stick into the computer. "I'm going with you. How do I know they won't do this to me next time?"

I looked at her. It was a wonderful sentiment, but I didn't want anything to happen to her. Besides, if I failed, I needed someone to finish the job—you know, avenge me and all that crap. I was about to protest when she nodded at me defiantly. Fine. There would be three of us. That would be enough for the punishment I would mete out to Richie and the Council. Now I just needed a plan.

CHAPTER THIRTY-THREE

"Assassination has never changed the history of the world."
—Benjamin Disraeli

The doorbell rang. I didn't even have to look at the monitors to know that Carolina Bombay was standing on my porch. Why was it I could always sense when she was going to call, or show up, or embarrass me in an Italian restaurant?

"Mom." I swung the door open. "Go home."

She pushed past me. "Like hell I will! It's my fault Romi's gone!"

Okay. She had me there. Not that I think she willingly served Romi up with a smile and even offered gas money to the kidnappers, but I did want to know what had happened.

So, Mom and I joined Liv and Dak in the kitchen.

"It was Lou," Mom started. "I always hated that son-of-a-bitch." This kind of salty language raised my eyebrows, but I didn't interrupt.

She took a long drink of beer, and I thought that hell must truly have frozen over, but I still didn't interrupt. "I answered the door and he came in, telling me you were in trouble with the Council, Gin. Your father was out walking Poppy, and Romi and I were making Halloween cookies—she said she needed them for school." I winced, silently vowing to stop Vivian once and for all when this was over.

"I shouldn't have turned my back on him," she continued. "That's when he got me. He always was a backstabber. Never could look you in the face, the slimy old fart." She took another drink of beer, draining the bottle. "When I came to, Romi was gone and there was a note saying the Council was taking her. So what I want to know is, what the hell is going on and when are we leaving to get my granddaughter?"

I looked at my mother. In her white blouse with a Peter Pan collar and long denim jumper, she looked like she belonged in a Hallmark ad. No one would ever suspect she was the woman who once had taken out a whole drug cartel in Colombia. In one sitting, no less.

"Mom," I said, "you can't go with us. Dak, Liv and I are going."

Liv piped up, "I'm going to call Paris. That'll be four of us."

Dak nodded. "Really, Mom. You need to stay here."

Suddenly, the Hallmark ad got scary as Mom's face turned grim. "Tell me what's going on."

So we told her. Come on. You can't lie to your mother about a thing like this. And we really didn't want her to go.

"If Richie's behind this, I'll bet Lou's involved too," Mom said quietly. "No one takes my granddaughter and lives."

I shuddered. My own mom creeped me out. Even with the Mary Englebreit wardrobe. Or maybe because of the Mary Englebreit wardrobe.

"I don't care if anyone else is involved. You're staying here." Have you ever tried to go up against your mother? Well, it ain't easy. But I put on my Sunday best steely resolve and stared her down.

Carolina looked at each of us for a moment, then sighed. "Fine. But if anything goes wrong, I'm taking them all out. Painfully. Slowly. Real Spanish Inquisition-like." Something in her voice gave me involuntary shivers. But I nodded and Mom finally left.

She wasn't gone ten minutes before the doorbell rang again. I rolled my eyes, but Liv caught me.

"It's Paris." She answered the door and then there were four of us.

Granted, we weren't the Magnificent Seven, but I thought we'd do all right. After all, we were younger and stronger than the Council. And a five-to-four ratio was pretty good odds. We sat down and started working out our plan.

An hour later, we took a break, and the others went home to get their gear, flashlights, guns and anything else they would need for the trip. Liv arranged for a private jet out of St. Louis so we wouldn't be tracked. Troy had hacked into all of the airlines' systems a few years back, so they'd be watching for us. And something told me that airport security would be a bit concerned to see four of us dressed ninja-style and armed to the gills with more weapons than you'd find at a Hezbollah-Hamas ice cream social.

I got dressed quickly, then hit my lab to get my Glock .45. As I closed the door, I looked down the hall at Romi's room and my blood chilled. I took one look inside, taking in the pink and purple room filled with stuffed animals, toys and books. On her dresser, I spotted an old picture of Ed. My throat closed up and started to ache. She had been just a baby when he died. It would've killed him to know who I was and what Romi was supposed to become.

Romi had never known her father. But this photo had a place of honor in her room. I blinked back the tears and looked at the ceiling, wondering how in the hell I was going to pull this off. As I closed the door, I hoped that Ed would forgive me for all I'd done and for what I was about to do.

The doorbell rang as I hit the first floor and I answered it without checking the monitors, figuring it was Dak, Liv or Paris. Imagine my shock when I found Diego standing there.

He looked me up and down. I must have been a weird sight, decked out in black from head to toe.

"Going somewhere?" he asked calmly, but I thought I detected something else in his voice.

"Diego, if you've come back to put more salt in the wound, I'd tell you I deserved it and open another vein for you to use. But this is a bad time."

He pushed past me into the hallway. "No, Gin. I just wanted to talk."

I was at a loss for words. It never occurred to me I'd see him again.

"I'm sorry, Diego, for everything. I never should have said those rotten things. I really didn't set you up. I would never do that to you. I meant it when I said I love you. But I completely understand how you must feel." My words came out Gatling-gun style.

"I didn't come here to yell at you or lecture you," he said slowly. "I came back because I want to try to understand this. I didn't think you really meant what you said."

The tears started, and I couldn't stop them. That's right, I was a crybaby assassin. And this was the right conversation, just at the wrong time. My relationship with Diego had to take a backseat to the life of my daughter.

"Diego, it's Romi. The Council has her at Santa Muerta. They won't hurt her if I turn Dak over to them." I ran my fingers through my hair as if that would make any of this easier. Actually, all it did was mess up my hair.

He stopped sharply, his face stony and hard. "What do you mean, they took Romi?"

I managed to fill him in before the others arrived. Once they saw Diego, Liv and Dak waved sheepishly at him, fumbling out a greeting. There were some awkward introductions once Paris arrived.

"So, you're all assassins?" he asked solemnly. Not knowing what else to do, Liv, Paris and Dak nodded.

Diego looked at our clothes. "I'm going with you."

I wanted him to. I mean, I really, really wanted him to. But it didn't seem right for an outsider to get mixed up in the Bombay mess.

I shook my head. "No. You can't. You're not even supposed to know any of this stuff. They'll kill you just for being an outsider."

Diego placed his hands on my shoulders, forcing me to look into his eyes. "I'm going with you. No one messes with my family."

Had he just said we were his family? I toyed with swooning, but there was no time.

"I'm going," he repeated. "Don't even try to talk me out of it."

"Okay," I finally agreed.

The five of us piled into my minivan (sounds like the beginning of a joke, *Four assassins and a bodyguard get into a minivan . . .*) and drove to Diego's hotel, where he changed into dark clothing. The others accepted Diego's presence with a sort of awe. I figured it was hard for them to imagine an outsider wanting to get involved. And it brought the ratio to one to one.

It took us a couple of hours to get to St. Louis. During that time, Dak filled Diego in on the island, the Council, and the most embarrassing stories he could think of regarding my childhood. You'd think there'd be a statute of limitations on how much mileage you can get out of a story where I ran naked through the streets at age six with a cereal bowl on my head.

Somehow, during this trip, we managed to come up with a cunning plan. We boarded our private jet, freaking out the pilot. We were delayed a few moments while we reassured him we weren't terrorists, ninjas, monochromatic mimes or anarchist beatnik poets. We knew what we had to do. But best of all, Diego was there, rushing into the fray alongside us, to save a little girl he considered family. Sigh.

CHAPTER THIRTY-FOUR

"I've got a cunning plan . . ."
  —Baldric, *Blackadder*

We landed in Ecuador at eight a.m. It didn't take long to find a speedboat to take us to Santa Muerta. We didn't rent it, just bought it outright, as there was the slight chance it might be destroyed in the rescue. I still wasn't convinced that there wasn't an explosive device implanted inside me. With my family, you could never be too paranoid.

The trick to landing at Santa Muerta was to enter the island where they wouldn't expect us. I mean, I knew they were expecting us, but it would be in our best interest to hide from the Council for as long as possible. Paris claimed he knew of a hidden cove near the bungalows, and after we all looked at him curiously, we set out.

By this point, Diego and Dak had become mates, as they say in Australia. I watched the two of them together, marveling at the differences and similarities. Diego was taller and more muscular than my brother. His wavy dark hair stood in contrast to Dak's blond, prep-school haircut. Diego moved like he'd seen combat, while Dak had a young, cocky self-assurance about him.

And yet, the two got along like twins. Before I started to compare them and feel icky that maybe I was dating a type like my brother, I turned my attention to the island in the distance.

It occurred to me that I've never tried to enter Santa Muerta clandestinely before. The island was strewn with booby traps, but as kids, we had played in and around them. Getting past security wasn't my main concern. It was how we'd pull it off when we got to the main building.

I didn't want to risk anything happening to Romi. I didn't think the Council would use her as a human shield, but then I never thought they'd use her as bait either. What had I learned from this mess? Never underestimate your family. Good advice.

I also didn't want anything to happen to Diego. He was an outsider, and this wasn't even his fight. Plus, I wanted a future with him. The Council would be much harder on his presence than ours.

No one from the outside had ever set foot on the island before. I was breaking every family rule.

Screw the rules. I came here to punish these bastards once and for all. But when it came down to it, would I really kill my own family? Yeah. I could do that. And in my mind's eye, they asked for it when they took an innocent little girl.

The wind ruffled my hair and the engine roared like it was desperate to see some action too. All five of us stared ahead, frowns of grim determination on our faces.

The family in this boat was what family was about. People who'd lay down their lives for you and yours. People who take care of each other. Not people who plot against each other. Maybe Richie knew a little about what he was doing. I patted my backpack, reassuring myself of the evidence lodged there.

Whoa. What was I thinking? Richie was a good guy? No. He had set up Dak and me to take a fall. He'd plotted to turn the family over to the authorities. But something in his thinking wasn't so foreign. While I doubted his motive was altruistic in any way, he wanted (for whatever reasons) to break up the family's vocation of dealing in death.

I shook my head to clear it. Don't worry. Richie was going down in a big way. But I had started to recognize that I wasn't interested in being part of the Bombay Family anymore. I wanted the people in the boat to be my family, but not those I was rushing to meet.

I caught Diego looking at me with what I assumed was curiosity. I sent him a weak smile and he rewarded me with a full, warm, genuine one. Diego didn't know it, but he was already a part of me. He loved Romi, and he loved me. No matter what, I vowed I would make it all up to him.

Paris slowed the engine and I could see we were coasting to a small, vine-covered cove about 200 yards to the west of the bungalows. As we pulled in, we lifted the veil of green and managed to tie up the boat behind a canopy of foliage.

"There's a small cave over there," Paris pointed, "where I used to hide out."

We all slowly turned to look at him.

Paris blushed. "I just needed a spot to be alone sometimes."

Dak asked, "Why?"

"To write poetry, okay? I always wanted to be a poet!" Paris blustered, then looked away.

"Leave him alone, Dak!" I smacked my brother up one side of the head. "Where does the cave go?"

Paris regained some of his composure, but now I imagined him in a white, billowy tunic, a jerkin and long boots.

"The cave actually lets out by the ropes

course. I'm pretty sure no one knows about it. It's always filled with undisturbed cobwebs and I've never seen any footprints in the mud. Not even last week. The best part is, we'll bypass the booby traps."

Liv and I looked at each other. She shrugged as if to say she'd had no idea her brother moonlighted as a bard.

"Sounds great." I took the lead. "It's a small island. But this should help us advance unannounced. Let's go."

The sun was up, but soon we ventured into complete darkness. We switched on our flashlights and followed Paris through a dark, dank tunnel covered in bat shit. I have no idea how long we walked.

No one spoke while we moved, just in case there was an echo. If the Council had other family members doing recon or was using some of Missi's devices to find us, we weren't going to make it easier.

Eventually, we emerged through a hole in the side of a cliff. Gulping as much fresh air as we could, we slowly made our way to the jungle floor. If Paris were right, the main building was a fifteen-minute hike to the east.

Paris was wrong. It took only ten minutes, tripping us up when we suddenly walked out of the fauna and into the pool area. The sun was directly above us, and we stood out like, well like assassins in black at a tropical pool party. No one was there, but I knew that security cameras were picking us up. They suddenly knew where we were. We had to act quickly to keep the Council off guard.

I ran to the door and opened it. Well, I guessed there were no surprises now. And the five of us burst into the Brutus Conference room, guns a blazin'.

The Council members sat in their seats on the dais, looking serenely at us as if we were scheduled to join them for tea. Not one of them reacted to the weapons in our hands. That kind of freaked me out, because we looked pretty scary, or so I thought.

"You're early," Grandma said tersely.

"Are you surprised?" I stepped in front of everyone else.

"Who's he?" Lou barked, pointing at Diego.

"Where's Romi?" I replied.

"I said, who is he?" Lou roared.

I leveled my gun, sights lining up in the middle of Lou's forehead. "He's my boyfriend. You got a problem with that?"

The Council exchanged looks, but still failed to fall to their knees in terror, begging for mercy. Damn.

"Where the hell is my daughter, Grandma?" I repeated.

"Where the hell is the mole, Virginia?" she responded. Damn. I hated it that she sounded cooler swearing than I did.

"I'm sure Richie is around here somewhere. He's next on my list. But age before beauty. Right?"

I heard the other pistols come up, each leveled at the forehead of a different Council member. I felt a surge of adrenaline. Now this was more like it!

"Richie is the mole?" Dela asked, her voice full of doubt.

I nodded. "Yes. Oh. Are you surprised, Aunt Dela?"

Lou stood and snorted. "Richie isn't the mole! He's saved us. Just like he saved you at the reunion."

Okay, so I lost a little of my composure. "He didn't save me! It's his fault I choked on the sponge cake! He wasn't even doing the Heimlich maneuver right!" I waved my gun around while I spoke. Behind me came noises of movement and I realized I'd left the agreed-upon course of action.

"Dak is the mole. And it's a good thing you brought him, or Romi wouldn't be going home with you." Lou sneered. I swear. He actually sneered.

"No, Uncle Lou. It's Richie. We have proof. But please excuse me if we don't set up a little PowerPoint presentation for you right now. You'll just have to take our word for it." I looked at Dak, whose pistol was pointed at Lou. "I think you should sit down and shut up before my brother blows your head off."

Lou sat down, glowering at me. Something was wrong. None of them were armed, nor were they making a move to defend themselves. Why? We could kill them all right now and there was nothing they could do about it. I'd already instructed everyone to aim for the head, just in case they had body armor on. What was going on?

"We know the truth, Gin," Troy said coldly. "Richie told us that the four of you were plotting against the family. He said you had incriminating photos of us. Is that true?"

Well, he had me there on the incriminating photos. In fact, they were in my backpack as we spoke. "No." Hello? Why weren't Liv or Dak speaking up? Hearing nothing from them, I continued, "That's not true. Richie took the pictures. He planted evidence on Dak in order to frame him. I want the mole dead as much as you do. But that mole is Richie, not us."

"I don't think so, Gin." Richie's voice came over the PA system. I could hear him, but I couldn't see him. He must have been in the multimedia booth. I fired a shot at the window.

"She shot me!" Richie screamed. "That bitch shot me!"

I got him? Huh. Didn't expect that. I really didn't think he'd be that stupid. Oh well. Yay me!

To my surprise, Diego walked to the control booth, kicked in the door (looking soooooo cool when he did that) and dragged my slimy little cousin out. By George, I *had* shot him! Just in the right thigh, but I finally got to shoot Richie!

I re-trained my gun on Grandma as Diego dropped my bleeding cousin in front of me, then returned to his position of targeting Troy.

"Thanks, hon!" I whispered as he walked past me. Diego grinned with amusement.

Time to get a confession out of Richie. "Tell them, dickhead. Tell them what you did before I shoot your balls off." I trained my gun on an area of Richie I didn't even want to think about.

"Owwwww!" Richie screamed. "She shot me!"

I rolled my eyes and kicked him, then pressed my boot down on his throat. "Tell them!"

"That's enough, Virginia!" Grandma barked. She rose and reached behind her chair, pulling my gagged-and-bound five-year-old forward in front of her. Romi's eyes grew wide as she saw her mother, aunt and uncles dressed like a SWAT team with guns aimed in her direction.

"You can have your daughter when you

turn Dak over to us. Give us the evidence and we will sort it out to decide what is going on."

I heard a sharp intake of breath behind me. "Gin, I'll go. They'll see. You have to get Romi back. They won't hurt me," Dak's voice pleaded behind me.

I turned to look at him in amazement. He loved Romi—that was never in doubt. And this was such an unselfish act, I wanted to hug him.

"Not a chance, Grandma," I shouted back. "Not much of a grandmother, are you? Kidnapping your great-granddaughter in order to kill your grandson. I don't think you should look for any more cards from us on Mother's Day."

Liv said, "We've seen the evidence. You'll just have to take our word for it. Now hand over Romi or this will be your last day on the Council."

Woo. Tough words. I liked it.

"Hell," Dak responded, "this will be your last day on the planet."

Grandma's jaw dropped. "You, my own grandchildren, would actually shoot me?"

We nodded in unison. "That's what you've trained us to do, isn't it?"

Grandma stamped her foot. "Fine." She began to untie Romi. "I wasn't really going to hurt her." Maryland walked my daughter over to me. "Let's see this evidence."

I lowered my gun and Romi kicked her

great-grandmother in the shins. Hard.
Twice. And while most children would be
punished for something like that, I figured it was time to raise her allowance
and give her a later bedtime. Good girl. I
pulled her behind me and she climbed
into Diego's arms.

I sighed wistfully, then tossed my backpack to Liv. "See if you can get this running in the media booth." I watched as
she lowered her gun from Florence, who
had remained strangely silent throughout
this, and walked over to the booth.

Grandma returned to her spot on the
stage, and I took my foot off Richie's
throat. I trained my gun on him. I'm not
completely hopeless.

Liv popped up in the window, frowning.
Through the PA system she announced,
"It doesn't work. I've got nothing on the
memory stick or the recording device."

Richie wheezed out a laugh. "Of course
not. We set up a strong electromagnetic
pulse in all the doorways. Your evidence
was deleted the minute you entered the
building." He started to laugh again, so I
kicked him in the thigh, causing an impressive blood spurt.

Dela folded her arms. "How convenient
that you don't actually have any proof. Are
we just supposed to believe you now?" As
if on cue, all five Council members pulled
pistols from behind their backs. Where

the hell had they come from?

We held our guns in place. It was a classic Mexican standoff. And with my family's marksmanship record, we could take each other out in one rapid burst.

Think, Gin, I pleaded with myself. No evidence. And we all have guns trained on each other. There was no way we could survive this. Sure, maybe one or two of us could, but not all of us. Liv came down from the booth, aiming at Florence.

"Drop them, Gin," I heard Lou say. "We have a lot more experience than you do. Put down your weapons and we'll talk about this like reasonable adults."

"Reasonable adults?" I shouted. "What kind of reasonable adults do this kind of crap? I think this family went beyond reasonable about two thousand years ago."

"Nonetheless, we will shoot you all, including Romi." Troy said calmly. *Limey peasant-fucker.* From now on—if we survived this—that's what I'd call him at the family reunions.

"Yeah, but we have a little problem," Liv said. "We don't trust you and you don't believe us. How are we going to work that one out? On the ropes course?"

I laughed. Even though we were in dire straits, it was pretty funny.

"How long do you think you can keep those guns on us?" Dela asked.

Grandma spoke up. "Lower your weapons and we'll give you a chance to prove yourselves. If not, I guarantee that most of you won't be going home."

For some reason, that music from Final Jeopardy started playing in my head. Unfortunately, the wrong answer in this case wouldn't just get us sent home with fabulous prizes.

I froze. Turning to look behind me would have given the Council the opportunity they needed. There was no way to consult with my troops. And Grandma was right. They would most likely take out at least three or four of us. The only advantage we had was that we were younger and could probably hold the guns up longer—at least that's the way things were looking with the geriatric hit squad and their trembling triceps.

I didn't trust them. But there was a chance they were telling the truth. Would they give us the opportunity to prove our innocence? I mean, it looked pretty bad with us in black, holding guns and all. But I could probably stand on Richie's head until he confessed. I'd even enjoy it.

But what if we lowered our weapons and they shot us? Granted, I was pretty sure Mom and Uncle Pete would avenge us, but what good was that? I didn't know if the Council could afford to take out four of its hitters. It would, at the very least, increase the retirement age.

The decision was an impossible one. It's like I came to a fork in the road, and just sat down, unable to decide. Could I wait it out? Not likely, judging by the tremors in Uncle Lou's hand. No, there was more of a chance that one of them would accidentally squeeze one off, launching quite a gun battle.

If we shot it out, some of us would die. If we did what they said, there was a slim chance we would all live. And I was starting to shake too. Where was a Magic 8 ball when you needed one?

CHAPTER THIRTY-FIVE

"You and I have unfinished business."
—The Bride, *Kill Bill*

"All right," I said, lowering my gun. "We'll trust you."

I turned and watched as Dak, Diego, Liv and Paris did the same. Romi stood behind Diego, looking really pissed off.

I took a deep breath. Here it was, our moment of truth. Would they keep their end of the agreement? Or was I about to join the family plot on the far side of the island?

Shit. The Council still had their guns trained on us. This was it. I was never going to marry Diego, see Romi grow up, or make those damned Halloween cookies. I closed my eyes, accepting my fate like a Bombay should.

I waited for the sound of the bullet that would soon be drilling through my head. Instead, there was a *zzzzzzt*. Like the sound of a large bug hitting a bug zapper. I opened my eyes and saw Missi standing in front of the stage, holding a small remote with a large red button. Why is it always a red button? Why not a blue one? Or yellow? Yellow would be good.

Even more amazing, the bodies of the Council members lay on the dais, twitching.

"You electrocuted them?" I asked Missi as Dak, Diego and Paris snatched up the Council's weapons.

Missi looked at the remote, a little distracted. "Oh yeah. I knew something like this might happen someday. So I implanted each of them with a device that sends a shock of electrical current. They're not dead. Just stunned."

"Huh. I always thought they had us implanted with explosives."

Missi arched her eyebrow. "That's paranoid."

I pointed to the dais. "You did it to them!" I scratched my chin. "How'd you do it?"

Missi laughed. "I told them all I was taking their measurements for more biometric technology. I," she lifted her hands to do finger quotes, "'accidentally' stuck them with a pin while taking their measurements. The pin released a mechanism into the elbow. They were totally clueless." She sighed. "Well, until now, that is. Of course, I knew something like this would happen someday."

I stared at her. "You knew this would happen?"

"I live here. I know how they think." She scowled at the twitching body of her grandmother, Dela. "That really pisses me off. Pulling guns on my cousins." She turned back to me. "We're family. We have to stick together."

Liv draped her arms around Missi and me. "Looks like Missi had our back."

I turned to hug Romi, when I spied, with my little eye, Richie dragging himself toward the door. I picked him up by the hair and hauled him back. "You aren't going anywhere." I looked at Missi. "All of our evidence is screwed. How are we going to prove he did it?"

"Well." Missi thought for a moment. "I think I can fix your stuff. If that doesn't work, you could always pull his fingernails out with pliers until he confesses." Her gaze turned to Richie. "Damn. I always hoped I'd be the one to nail him. Nice shootin', Tex."

Diego, Dak and Paris had revived the Council, helping them back into their chairs. We tied them up. I'm not a total moron.

It didn't take long for Missi to get the bugs worked out of our equipment. We made the Council listen to the tape and look at the photos. In the end, they agreed that Richie had, in fact, been behind it all.

Once they were untied, the Council asked me to drag Richie to the front of the room.

"Virginia," Grandma began, "the Council apologizes for putting you and Romi through this. We were wrong. You may not know this, but in such situations, the Council has to allow you certain concessions." She looked at Richie, bleeding and whining on the stage. "One of them being, you get to take him out as your reward."

I looked at my cousin, then back at the Council. I couldn't tell you how long I'd wanted to kill him. Especially since he'd been responsible for terrorizing my family. Hell, if it had gone according to his plan, Dak or Romi and possibly I would be dead. He didn't deserve to live. I finally had the satisfaction of showing the family what an ass he was.

"What kind of concessions?" I asked the Council.

"Well, ahem," Lou sputtered. "You get one demand of your choosing."

I turned and looked at my brother, my cousins, my daughter and the love of my life.

"I don't want anything to happen to Diego. I brought him here. And I plan to make him part of the family. You cannot punish him for being an outsider."

Liv, Dak and Paris nodded and Romi flung her arms around Diego. I turned back to the Council.

"Richie, as much as I've always wanted to take you out, I'm going to refuse this particular concession. I really don't want to do this anymore. The Council can take care of you. But I don't want any part of it." I gave him a right cross to the jaw. "And you didn't save my life at the reunion." He slumped to the floor, unconscious.

The members of the Council looked at each other in surprise. Our family had been so well-trained in the arts of "correcting" the black sheep, my refusal to kill Richie stunned them.

"Virginia." Grandma spoke up again, nodding to the fellow Council members. "For your gesture and support, and the fact that you didn't kill us, the Council grants you early retirement from the family business. Effective immediately."

To say I was shocked would be an understatement. I waited to react, just in case the others didn't agree. To my surprise, they all nodded.

I turned and ran into Diego's arms. He crushed me in his embrace, then pulled Romi up into a group hug. I couldn't believe it! I was retired! Which meant I got the guy! Which meant everything would be okay! Whew! Good thing I didn't shoot Richie dead!

The others joined us in a huge embrace and we laughed until we cried. Even some of the Council members smiled a little. I turned to Missi and gave her the thumbs-up. She was holding a gun on Richie with a blissed-out look on her face. So she was going to get the prize. That was great. She had certainly earned it.

It only took a few hours to call our jet to pick us up from the island to take us home. I spent the whole time in Diego's arms with Romi on my lap. Dak found some Moet and Chandon White Star champagne on board and we all drank ourselves silly.

"Diego?" Romi asked solemnly.

He pulled her onto his lap. "What is it, princess?"

"Will you marry us?"

Diego looked from me to her, then kissed her on the cheek, "Of course I will. If your mum will have me, that is."

"Oh, I'll have you," I whispered amongst the cheers of my family, "again, and again, and again."

EPILOGUE

"That was the best vacation ever! I love our family."
—Dash, The Incredibles

"Mrs. Bombay?" Kaitlyn looked up at me. "Is this right?"

"Pretty good." I took her hand in mine and led her through the motions. "You need to release the knife a little bit later. That will help improve your aim."

Kaitlyn did just as I asked and nailed the target, dead center. I was so proud of her.

"Girls!" Liv shouted. "Snack time!"

In seconds she was surrounded by ravenously hungry Daisies. While she doled out the cookies and milk, I pulled the knives out of the board that served as our target. After carefully wiping them off, I slid them back into their leather cases and stuck them on my belt.

Mom waved from the porch, and I walked over to take another tray of cook-

ies to the girls. It was really sweet of her
to let us use her yard.

Actually, the meetings had been going
very well. There were no more incidents
with pipe cleaners and glue. In fact, the
girls had taken to their new training with
a military precision that surprised me.

And while the Girl Scout Council (the
only council I answer to these days—and
much less lethal) thought they were too
young for the archery training, throwing
knives and using chemistry sets to make
explosives, the Scouts were having one
hell of a good time. I'm planning a trip
next year to a survivalist camp. I think my
Daisies will love it.

Vivian wasn't saying much these days.
Maybe because I came through with the
Halloween cookies, or maybe because I
had a new, hunky Australian husband. I'd
like to think that it was because her
daughter (in my troop) now knew how to
make a simple car bomb using hair gel, a
cell phone and ammonia. I guess it didn't
really matter why she avoided me, just
that she kept doing it.

And you heard me right. Diego Jones
became Diego Bombay. We had to work
through some things once we got back,
but we managed. Now that I'd retired, he
felt he could accept the past and had long
since forgiven me for whacking Turner. In

fact, Diego retired too and we're living a
good life off Bombay blood money. So
everyone wins.

Diego and I had a simple Justice of the
Peace ceremony before Halloween and
then he moved in officially. You might
think our days were dull and quiet. What
with taking Romi to school in the morning, coming back home and having sex
until noon, taking a post-coital nap, picking up Romi, then doing family stuff until
bedtime (when there's more sex until we
fall asleep). But so far, we aren't bored
yet. Poppy finally became housetrained—
a major cause for celebration. Of course,
the little slut spends all her time on
Diego's lap.

There were no plans to visit Santa
Muerta in the near future, but we were going to Australia during the holidays to
meet Diego's family. As for my family, they
held a more important place in my heart
than ever. Liv and I were still training Romi
and Alta (couldn't get out of that one, unfortunately), and Grandma had sent each
of her grandchildren an American Express
Black Card with an unlimited line of credit
and a private concierge in each city, as a
form of apology. I was definitely not too
proud to use it. I even had sent a nice
thank-you note.

There were no secrets in my household
anymore. I opened up the secret work-

shop and turned it into a room for all my knitting stuff. Of course, I still keep up on the family business. Romi will be joining it one day and I want to be on top of things. Oh, and I had Missi scan my body for hidden explosives, just to be sure.

I guess you could say that what began with an invitation to a family reunion of assassins ended with a new family of my own. A much happier ending, I think.

Of course, from time to time, my mind wandered to the safe in my new knitting room. Where, in case you're wondering, I kept the photos. They might prove useful someday. With a family like the Bombays, I wasn't ruling anything out.

ATTENTION
BOOK LOVERS!

Can't get enough of your favorite **ROMANCE**?

Call **1-800-481-9191** to:

✳ order books,

✳ receive a **FREE** catalog,

✳ join our book clubs to **SAVE 30%!**

Open Mon.-Fri. 10 AM-9 PM EST

Visit **www.dorchesterpub.com**
for special offers and inside
information on the authors you love.

We accept Visa, MasterCard or Discover®.
LEISURE BOOKS ♥ **LOVE SPELL**